RETURNED TO THE BAY

Hannah Westley

Book Layout © 2017 BookDesignTemplates.com

Returned To the Bay/ Hannah Westley. -- 1st ed.
ISBN 9798330307098

Cover photo credit Eagleheadbluff

For Effie Lee Wilson, you are not forgotten. You live on in the words of this book and in the winds and the waves of the Chesapeake.

For Jeffrey, thank you for showing me what true love is, and for always encouraging and supporting me, I love you more than life.

Jen, for always having my back, and for fighting for me when I could not fight for myself. I appreciate and love you.

To Steven and Diane White, thank you for your efforts and courage in your attempts to save Holland Island. Your efforts do not go unnoticed or unappreciated.

CONTENTS

Prologue

Holland Island, August 1918. The wind swept gently through the island, winding through the trees and curling along the streets. The church, which had once stood as the pillar of strength in the center of town, was now damaged beyond repair. The hurricane that tore apart the island left very little standing. All of the homes that had once sat on the west side of the island were completely gone, sliding and crumbling, surrendering to the bay. The streets, shops, and homes that remained were empty and silent.

Chapter One

Hattie 1917

There was a chill in the air on the morning of October 1st, 1917, the first day of oyster season. Hattie reluctantly opened her eyes to the sun slowly moving up her windowpane. Oyster season was one of the busiest times on the island. Sloops, schooners, and skipjacks filled the Chesapeake Bay, with fishermen dredging from sunup to sundown. The oyster population on the coastlines up north had grown scarce due to mass harvesting, causing a high demand for oysters from the Chesapeake Bay in southern Maryland. Thanks to the completion of the railroad, fishermen from the mainland and surrounding islands were taking advantage of this opportunity to make a living harvesting oysters. Hattie's father was a local fisherman who moved to Holland Island from Cambridge, Maryland, in 1896, shortly after marrying Hattie's mother. He saw this as an opportunity to start a life, build a family, and live comfortably from the benefits of the bay. He always talked about the bay with respect and gratitude, never taking for granted the value of the marine life that lived on the bottom of its waters. "It gives us everything we need," he told her more times than she could count. "And for that, we should always be grateful to the Bay."

Hattie spent many chilly mornings alongside her father harvesting oysters and had come to accept the way and rhythm of life on Holland Island. But today she didn't feel like it, today was her 18th birthday. She had heard of the Universities in the big cities, live music and dancing on the weekends, the grand parties and the gala's that girls her age were attending hoping to find eligible bachelors with top hats and wealthy families, and today she longed for that. *Just once,* she thought, just so she could experience what it would be like. She sat up and stretched her hands over her head, then slid the covers off and slowly stood, her head hanging low as she made her way to her dresser. She stared at her reflection in the mirror imagining herself in a full-length, satin gown that showed off her cleavage. Her sandy blonde hair would be tied up with a few trailing curls at the back of her neck, red lipstick on her plump, youthful lips and rosy blush on the ends of her cheekbones. She put one hand out and reached for the hand of her imaginary suitor, curtsied and swayed as if she'd been asked to dance. She twirled around her bedroom humming "Melody of

Love" by Tom Glazer and H. Engelmann and imagined that a tall, handsome man with deep blue eyes, dressed in a dark tailcoat, a winged collared shirt and bow tie, was holding her close and leading her around the room. The worn floorboards creaked and moaned as she spun in circles on her tippy toes; she was completely lost in her glamorous moment when she was suddenly snapped out of her imaginary world and back into her present life as her right pinky toe slammed into the corner of her bedpost.

"Blast!" she cried. "You stupid girl," she scolded herself as she rubbed her little toe, which now felt like it had its own heartbeat. *Better get dressed and get moving. Papa will be waiting,* she told herself as she stood and took off her nightgown, slid on her knee-high socks, a plain cotton dress that fell to her ankles, and slid on an oatmeal-colored cardigan that her mother had given her last year for Christmas. So plain, so boring she thought as she slid her arms through the sleeves.

"It's sensible and goes with anything," her mother had told her when she opened it on Christmas morning. But "sensible and goes with anything" is the last thing Hattie wanted to be.

Hattie's mother was Amelia Thomas, the heart and cornerstone of their family. Born just outside of Cambridge, Maryland in 1868, Amelia grew up on a farm with four brothers and two sisters. Most of her family still lived on farms in that area. After studying at

Cambridge University, she became a registered nurse, also becoming the first person in her family to earn a degree. In 1896, after college, Amelia's father fell ill and unexpectedly passed away. After graduating from college, Amelia found herself shouldering the responsibility of providing for her family after her father's sudden passing. She dedicated her days to bringing the bounty of fruits and vegetables to the market in downtown Cambridge. Meanwhile, Henry, a local, hardworking fisherman, lived with his father in a charming house nestled along the tranquil shoreline. One day, Henry stopped by Amelia's family farm stand and was instantly drawn to her beautiful smile. With his gentle nature and sincere kindness, he quickly captured her heart. After a few weeks of courtship, they got married and moved in with Henry's father along the shore.

Henry found the competition with other fishermen at the docks and the increasing population in Cambridge (over 4,000 residents) frustrating and impossible. Henry had heard of Holland Island, a small town with only about 280 residents, and decided it would be better for him and Amelia to move to the quaint, quiet island to start over and make a home of their own where he could fish and harvest oysters for a living. Amelia supported his decision and quickly gave up her dreams of using her degree and working in the healthcare field.

By 1910, the island had grown to about 360 residents, making it one of the largest inhabited islands in the Chesapeake Bay. It had 70 homes, a few stores, its own post office, a two-room schoolhouse with two teachers, a church, a baseball team, a community center, and a doctor.

However, life was changing on the small island. The Chesapeake Bay had slowly been encroaching on the land and homes on the west side of the island. Families had started packing up their homes and moving to the mainland, transporting their entire homes on barges, and had to start over somewhere else. Nonetheless, some families refused to give up on the island, risking it all to stay on the land where they had built their lives and families. Life was simple, quiet, and routine.

Amelia's love for routine and order kept a predictable and stable rhythm in their home. From organizing community church bike rides to making sure dinner was always hot and ready on the table at 5:30 pm, her mother always made sure it was done. While her mother seemed to thrive in the mundane and routine, Hattie felt suffocated by it. She never understood why her mother gave up her dream of working as a nurse at a hospital and settled for the quiet life here on the island.

What a waste, she thought. Hattie longed for adventure and yearned for something more, something different. Some days, she would stand on the shoreline, her bare feet in the water, the sun setting in front of her, and stare out across the bay, wondering what was beyond the horizon, what life was like somewhere else, anywhere else.

Hattie made her way down the stairs and into the kitchen where the smell of black coffee and biscuits hung in the air. Her younger brother Oliver, "Ollie" what they called him for short, was sitting at the table with a warm biscuit smothered in butter and strawberry jam. Hattie reached out with her hand to grab his freshly made breakfast.

"Don't you dare!" he snapped, but before he could stop her, she grabbed the biscuit and took a large bite. "Hattie!' he scolded. She smiled a childish grin, set what was left of the biscuit back on his plate and tousled his sandy blonde hair. "You're so annoying," he said in an agitated and defeated tone.

"Aww, I'm sorry, but it *is* my birthday," Hattie replied, with butter and jam smeared on the top of her lip and nose. Ollie lowered his head and looked up at her from the tops of his eyes,

"Fine," he moaned with his teeth tightly clenched together. "But don't do it again! You always take a bite of my food," he said in a tone that sounded more like her parents than her brother.

"Ok, I won't," she said with a grin as she crossed her fingers behind her back, knowing full well this wouldn't be the last time. "Did Momma already leave for the quilting circle?" she asked.

"Yeah, she left half an hour ago, and Pa already left for the skipjack. You better hurry if you're going to catch him."

She grabbed a rag off the sink and wiped her mouth. Slipped on her rubber boots and wool cap and left out the back door.

"Have a good day at school!" she hollered back at Ollie as she took off towards the dock.

Gray clouds hung low and full overhead; the air was thick with the smells of the bay. Fish, pondweed, crab, tall pond grass and cypress all mixed together creating a fragrant melody, a fragrance that she had smelled all her life and grown so familiar with; a fragrance that she barely noticed anymore. Tall tan grasses swayed with the wind, and seagulls' calls echoed against the water, giving a rhythmic tone to the air.

In the distance, pelicans took turns swooping down and plunging into the bay, filling up their pouch with water and herring fish. She noticed that they tilted their heads slightly to the right before they hit the water. She wondered why they did that and made a mental note to find out someday. She could see that her father had already left on the skipjack, she would have to wade in the shallow water and use the rake to collect the oysters. She slumped her shoulders and kicked at the dirt beneath her feet. She hated harvesting this way, her hands would get wrinkled and numb from reaching down into the cold water over and over again. When she walked, frigid, murky bay water would splash up and get inside her boots causing her socks to get wet. She could tolerate lots of annoyances, but wet socks were by far the worst.

"Happy birthday to me," she said sarcastically to herself as she reluctantly trudged to the shed to get the rake and crates. *"This is going to be a long day."* She grumbled under her breath.

Eden 1982

Eden's eyes popped open with the first sight of the sun's light; it was June 15th, today was her 18th birthday and she had been looking forward to this day all year. She and her best friend Melanie were taking Melanie's dad's boat out on the Chesapeake Bay to explore what was left of Holland Island. Eden had heard a few stories about the small island from her grandmother, but she never went into a lot of detail about her life there over 60 years ago. Eden had taken it upon herself and investigated the history of the island at the local library, reading newspaper clippings and looking at old photographs that were taken of the island back in its heyday. She had read stories about the families who had to pack up everything they'd owned and start over, even some of their homes were taken apart and shipped on barges to the mainland to be rebuilt, it seemed unimaginable. Eden's grandmother never expressed interest in going back to the island after leaving it all those years ago.

"There are some hurts not even time can heal, it only dulls the ache," her grandmother had told her whenever Eden asked her to go.

There was something about the island that drew Eden to it, she couldn't explain why, but she had always felt drawn to it, like there was an invisible string pulling her to it and was relentless in its quest to bring her to the island. And today she was finally going to see it with her own eyes. She threw off her blankets, changed out of her pajamas, and put on her light blue bikini, a pair of jean shorts, and a faded Led Zeppelin tee shirt, tied up her long sandy blonde hair, and headed down the stairs.

"Happy Birthday beautiful girl!" her mother said, holding a box of fresh donuts from the local bakery.

Eden smiled, "Thanks mom." She took the box of donuts from her and turned to slide on her flip-flops.

"You're not going to stay and eat them with me?" her mom asked in a sarcastic, sad tone.

"I don't want to be late, I told Melanie we would meet at her dock at 8:15 am and it's already 7:55, I'm sorry," Eden replied.

"I understand, you get going, but don't be late tonight! I have a birthday dinner planned," her mother said as she sat down on the sofa.

"I know I know, 6:30 right?" Eden asked.

"Yes, 6:30, and Melanie is welcome to join us if she wants," her mother replied.

"Ok, I'll tell her," Eden leaned down and kissed her mother on the cheek, then flew out the front door leaving it slightly open.

"Wear a life jacket!" her mother called out as she got up and closed the door. *My wild child*, she thought as she watched Eden take off towards Melanie's house on her bike with the box of donuts balancing on her knees.

Melanie's father's boat was a 1970 StarCraft Polaris 16' fiberglass boat with a 65 HP Evinrude outboard motor. It was nothing fancy, but according to Eden's calculations, it should get them to Holland Island in about an hour. Melanie lived in a small cottage-style home right on the bay in Ridge, Maryland. Eden lived just 2 miles up the road, a few streets away from the bay. The girls met in kindergarten over finger painting and have been inseparable ever since. Eden had been there for Melanie when her mother passed away from cancer when Melanie was only 9 years old. And likewise, Melanie had been there for Eden when her parents got a divorce when Eden was 8. They spent many hot summer days out on Melanie's dock, jumping in and out of the cool water. They'd pretend they were mermaids who ruled the Chesapeake Bay; the blue herons, loggerhead turtles, and blue shell crabs were the townspeople of their kingdom. Clam and snail shells were treasures that they'd find hidden in the earth and along the sandy shoreline. They would spend every summer day out in the water, exploring, playing, and sunbathing. Even as they got older, they still loved spending time in and by the water. Neither of them had a sister, so they cherished their close friendship, sharing everything from clothes and snacks to secrets and tears. They would tell people that they were sisters; they never fooled anyone because they looked nothing alike, but deep down the girls truly believed it. They promised each other that they would always stay close forever, no matter what happened or where they might end up. Neither one of them had made plans past high school yet but Melanie's father was starting to encourage her to look at colleges up north as far as Boston, Massachusetts. Eden's heart sank at the thought of her best friend being that far away. Eden had never wanted to leave her mother and grandmother and go to a college out of state. She loved her life on the bay and couldn't imagine saying goodbye to it.

Melanie was already on the boat, loading a small cooler with sandwiches and drinks, a mesh beach bag that had towels, a camera, and some snacks for their adventure. Melanie was taller than Eden, with long, dark brown, wavy hair that fell to her lower back. She had big brown eyes and a round face, she had a "happy-go-lucky" way of looking at life that Eden admired and loved.

"Hey girl!" Eden hollered in a playful tone as she approached the dock.

"Hey! Happy birthday!" Melanie squealed as she jumped off the boat and onto the dock, running towards her with excitement for the day ahead. She threw her arms around Eden and squeezed her tight. "Are you excited?" she asked Eden with her arms still wrapped around her neck.

"Yes! We've only been talking about it all year!" she said jokingly. The two girls let go of each other and headed toward the boat. "My mom bought us donuts, and she said you're welcome to come to my birthday dinner tonight too if you want," Eden said.

"Want to? I'd love to! I can't wait to talk to your grandma after this! I still can't believe she didn't want to come along?" Melanie said.

"I know, I guess it just brings up too many memories, too many hurts that she's tried to forget," Eden replied.

They stepped into the boat; Melanie took her place at the wheel while Eden untied the lines, threw them in the boat and jumped in. Melanie started up the boat's engine with a staggered stutter, water gurgling as the boat slowly headed away from the dock, and towards the open bay. The murky water lapped against the boat, encouraging the girls in their quest for adventure and the discovery of what was left of the desolate island. The seagulls squalled and called as they made their way across the bay and closed in on the remains of Holland Island.

Chapter Three

Hattie 1917

The sun was now high in the sky, taking the chill out of the autumn air. Hattie had been raking oysters for almost 5 hours filling a little over 8 crates. Her hands were wrinkled, numb, and calloused from picking oysters out of the water and tossing them in the crates, her stomach groaned, reminding her that it had been many hours since she had eaten anything. Seagulls flew around her in the distance squalling and squawking at each other.

"Be quiet, you noisy things!" she hollered, but they carried on with their songs of annoyance which seemed to grow louder as if in defiance to her request to be quiet. She picked up a rock and hurled it in their direction, missing them completely.

"Good throw," a voice said in a low, sarcastic tone. It startled her, causing her to jump and lose her balance, her foot slipped against the mossy rocks sending her tumbling into the chilly bay water. Her dress was soaked, her boots filled with water soaking her socks all the way to her knees. She turned and saw a young man sitting in a small fishing boat. He had a cotton shirt that was unbuttoned at the top revealing his chest that had been tanned by sunny days fishing on the bay.

"Excuse me?!!" she questioned him with an angry tone.

"I'm sorry," he said, trying not to laugh but was having a hard time containing himself. "I didn't mean to scare you and make you fall," he said through a childlike smile.

"You should be sorry. I'm soaked to the bone!" She said as she stood up, and wobbled again, almost losing her balance a second time. "It's rude to sneak up on a stranger and scare them." she continued.

"I didn't sneak up, I rowed over to you in my boat, in broad daylight, I'd hardly call that sneaking," he said, and let out a suppressed chuckle. She glared at him, as she took off her cardigan to wring it out. He paddled closer to her and jumped out of his boat. "Let me help you" he said kindly.

"No thank you," she snapped, "you've done enough already."

"I'm sorry, please let me help you," he reached out his hand to take her cardigan, and she handed it to him, dripping with water.

He twisted it, folded it in half, and twisted it again, getting most of the water out. She couldn't help but notice how the twisting motion showed off his strong hands and veiny forearms. She felt her face get flushed and looked away. He handed it back to her, "we could hang it up on the edge of my boat, let the sun dry it out."

"Thank you," she said in an agitated tone.

He noticed the crates full of oysters, "That's a pretty good haul you got there, oyster girl. How long have you been out here?"

Hattie glanced over at the crates and sighed "All day."

"Have you had anything to eat?" he asked.

"No, I was getting ready to go back home for some lunch right when you showed up and scared the dickens out of me." She said with a little smile, her tone less agitated and more friendly. He saw her smile and stared for a second, he couldn't help but notice the dimple on her cheek that showed up when she grinned.

"I have some lunch in my boat we could share. There's plenty, take it as my apology for scaring you half to death and making you fall" he offered.

She hesitated for a moment, but the thought of food made her stomach growl in acceptance. "Alright," she said as she rolled her eyes playfully.

They both walked over to his boat and climbed inside. He pulled out half a loaf of sourdough bread, some cheese, and a jar full of lump crab meat. He tore the bread in half and handed her a piece.

"Thank you," she said, her tone much softer now.

"You're welcome," he replied. The two of them sat and ate lunch in silence for a few minutes, taking in the sights and sounds around them. Seagulls flew overhead, waiting for a scrap of food to be offered, katydids chirped in the tall grasses of the marsh. The water gently lapped the side of the boat, making a soothing rhythm.

"So, how long have you lived on the island?" he asked.

"All my life," she replied, "I've never been any-where else," she said with a shrug of her shoulders.

"You say that like it's a bad thing," he said with a smile.

"Well, I feel like it is!" she replied abruptly, "I would love to go to the city, go to the opera, maybe even one of those big universities like some of my friends. Did you know that automobiles fill the streets in New York City? And at Christmas time they deco-rate the storefronts of the windows and line the treetops with Christmas lights! I knew a girl who got married to a banker and lives in a big, brick-row home in New York City now. Can you imagine how exciting her life must be?"

He didn't know girls could talk this much or this fast. He looked out at the bay, watching the waves lapping all around them. Silence hung in the air for a moment.

"Yeah, I guess, but I don't understand how anyone would want to leave a place like this," he said as he nodded towards the bay.

She looked around, her brows wrinkled, puzzled by his reply.

"This?" she said as she motioned towards the marshy shoreline, flinging her hand causing crumbs of bread to fly in the air, sending the seagulls into a squalling frenzy. "This swampy, fishy, crabby, bug-biting, seagull squawking, boring, old smelly island?" she questioned.

"Yes," he chuckled, as he looked down at his hands fumbling with a piece of bread. "To me, this place has the most beautiful sunsets that make the water glow in reds, pinks, and purples, the birds that sing their songs all year round, the fish that jump clear out of the water showing off their fat, silver bellies, the dragonflies with kaleidoscope of colors in their wings." His voice was low and rhythmic. He spoke with both wonder and reverence.

She stared at him for a moment, taking in his love and appreciation for this place, a place she so often resented and felt captive of, a place she felt like she would never be able to escape from. She looked around, as if looking with new eyes, taking in the beauty of the island that she had taken for granted so many times, trying to see it as if she were looking through his eyes.

She sighed.

"I still think the city would be better, more exciting."

He chuckled at her response, she was so forward, so blunt about how she felt, and this amused him.

"So why are you out here harvesting oysters and not at a big city school?" he asked.

"Helping my Pa, he hurt his back last year and hasn't been able to harvest as much. He said he'd give me a third of the profits from everything I bring in," she said with a smile. "I'm saving up my share to go to see a band play live music," she said in almost a whisper with a wry smile, her eyes as big as saucers.

"Oh yeah?" he mused.

"Mhm, the new jazz music is what I really want to see, have you heard it?" She asked. He shook his head.

"No I haven't,"

"Oh heavens! You absolutely must, they each play in their own rhythm, their own beat, it's purposeful, musical, chaos that's extremely captivating, it's like nothing I've ever heard before! And I'm going to go hear it live someday," she said as she sat up straight and held her head high like a peacock.

"Well good for you," he said with a grin.

A pelican dove into the water in the distance.

"You see that?" he asked, pointing to the spot where the pelican's body entered the water. "You see how he turned his head right before he hit the water?"

"Yes! Why do they do that?" she asked curiously.

"It's to protect their throat," he answered.

"Interesting," she replied in a whisper, amused by his answer. She looked at him, trying to understand him. He had a deep calmness, but also a wild curiosity for the nature and wildlife on the island that was so captivating. "How long have you lived on the island?" she asked him.

"I grew up on Smith Island, my father taught me fishing, crabbing, how to capture ducks and harvest oysters, but I left a few months ago and came here after the wardens from Virginia came over on patrol boats and killed him for harvesting oysters."

"Oh, my goodness!" she exclaimed. "I'm so sorry, how could they do such a thing?" she asked, her voice full of shock.

"My father was an oysterman, the government is putting laws in place that want to keep them from taking too much, and well, the islanders don't agree with that. How can man regulate what is given from God?" He paused, and then continued, "there've been quite a few men that have been wounded and killed fighting for what they feel ain't right," he said in a low voice, trying to conceal the pain, his eyes looking out at the bay. She looked at him, feeling a sense of empathy and compassion. "I didn't want to end up like that," he continued, "so I packed up what I had and came over to Holland Island. I met an old man named Tom Wilson. He lives over on the other side of the island. He's been real kind. I help him tie his nets, scale fish, and build crab traps. In return, he gives me a place to stay."

He took a bite of cheese and then threw a piece out to the gulls. They both chuckled as they watched the wild birds scramble and fight each other for the small scrap of food.

The sun was beating down hotter now, so Hattie took off her wool cap and set it down on the seat in the boat and shook out her long blonde hair. It fell in loose waves around her shoulders, combing it through with her fingers. He couldn't help but stare at her, like something he'd never seen before. He stared at her like she was a fine piece of art that deserves to be admired and studied. She stopped when she caught him staring at her.

"Why are you looking at me like that?" she asked.

"Because you're beautiful, probably the most beautiful girl I've ever seen," he replied with a confidence that even surprised him.

She threw her head back and laughed out loud. "You can't be serious!... Me?" she replied.

"Yes. You, oyster girl. You're so, so refreshing. You're like new snow that covers the ground in the winter, stunning." He said with a softness in his voice.

She laughed again, "My, my, aren't you quite the poet, a real charmer," she said chuckling.

"No, I'm not," he said as he held up his hands in protest, "I swear, I'm not like that, it's just," he fumbled over his words now and his face turned red. "You're not like the other girls, you're different, authentic. You're like a pearl hidden in an oyster," he paused trying to find the right words to say, "The extraordinary hidden among the ordinary, that's what you are." He smiled and paused, waiting for her to say something.

She smiled, looked him in the eyes.

"And you are crazy."

He chuckled and looked down at his feet with an embarrassed grin. "But you're sweet," she said as she smiled.

They sat in silence for a moment. Then she heard a man holler her name in the distance,

Hattie sighed. "That's my Pa, I better get going." She jumped out of the boat, grabbed her cardigan and rake and started heading towards her crates full of oysters. "Thanks for lunch!" she hollered at him.

"You're welcome, oyster girl" he replied.

"My name is Hattie, by the way," she said with a bit of sass.

He smiled, "Pleased to meet you Hattie, I'm Wesley, but you can call me Wes,"

"Alright then, bye Wes. I'll see you around?" she asked with a smile.

"Yes ma'am, I hope so," he said with a grin that took over his whole face. He slowly started rowing away, watching her slowly fade from view as she hoisted up the oyster crates and started to head back home. He looked down and saw that she had left her wool cap in his boat, he smiled and picked it up, he held the soft cap in his hand, smoothing his thumbs over the wool. *Hattie the oyster girl, the most beautiful girl in the world,* he thought.

Chapter Four

Eden 1982

They spotted it in the distance; it stuck out of the water like a foreign object, a haunting reminder of what was and what was no more, the last house on Holland Island. The white paint was faded and chipped, weathered from years of wind and rain. Cracked and broken windows framed a hollow, darkness within. The foundation strained to hold on, begging for one more day above the surface of the bay, pleading to all who passed by as if to say, "Don't forget about me, don't forget about the island." Pelicans sat perched on the peak of the rooftop, guardians of what belonged to them now, the only residents left on the deserted marshland. A hush fell over them as Melanie killed the motor, tall grasses swayed in the breeze welcoming them to the abandoned shore. Eden and Melanie's breath seemed to stand still within their chests as the boat grew closer to the marshy shoreline. Eden jumped out into the water below. The bay water reached her thighs as she pulled the boat up to the shore.

Melanie jumped out and stood beside Eden.

"This is crazy" she said, breaking the silence that had fallen over them since they first spotted the island.

"Yeah it is, I wasn't expecting to feel so, so..." Eden's voice trailed off, looking for the word.

"Sad?" Melanie said in a knowing tone.

"Yeah, sad," Eden replied.

The two of them walked towards the house, stepping over driftwood and rocks, pushing through tall grasses and swampy ground as they made their way to the dilapidated house. They reached the front of the house, just remnants of what once were the front steps that led to the large, whitewashed front door. Eden looked around at the scenery and couldn't help but imagine what it would be like to live here.

"It's so beautiful," she said in almost a whisper.

"Yeah, it is, it's unreal" Melanie added.

"I want to see inside; can you lift me up?" Eden asked.

"I can try!" Melanie said. Melanie interlocked her fingers with both her hands and bent down so Eden could step on them. Melanie lifted her up, Eden grabbed the bottom ledge of the front windowsill, the peeling paint chipped off under her fingertips. She held on and peered through the dusty window.

"I see a table with chairs and old jars and cans!" She exclaimed.

"Yeah?" Melanie grunted, feeling the weight of Eden's body.

"There's a bookshelf too!" Eden said.

"What are you two doing?" a male voice said in a surprised tone.

Both girls screamed, Melanie lost hold of Eden's foot, causing Eden to come down on top of her, both girls toppled and fell, one on top of the other onto the marshy ground. They both looked up in surprise and saw a young man who looked to be a year or two older than they were. He had windblown light brown hair and hazel eyes. He wore a backwards baseball hat, faded blue tee shirt, above the knee jean shorts with a flannel long sleeve shirt tied around his waist and rubber boots.

"We just came to explore the island." Eden said as she rolled off Melanie and stood up, patting off the grass that had taken hold on the backside of her shorts.

"What are you doing here?" Melanie questioned from her seat on the marsh floor.

"I come here all the time. I pretty much own the island. I know every inch of it," he replied confidently.

"Oh, really?" Melanie asked with a tone that was drenched in sass.

"Yeah, really. My grandfather lived here a long time ago, he told me all about this place. I came here with him all the time as a kid," he replied.

Melanie stood to her feet annoyed.

"Well just because your grandfather lived here, doesn't make you the owner of it," she scolded.

"Wait! Your grandfather lived here?" Eden said, cutting off Melanie's words as she pushed past her and stepped closer to him.

"Yeah, he did. He was 19 when he first came here, he was born on Smith Island, he was a fisherman," he answered.

"My grandmother lived here. She lived here her whole life until she was 18. Her and her family moved because of all the erosion," Eden said.

"Yeah, pretty crazy, isn't it? Everyone eventually left because of it. I wonder if your grandma knew my grandpa?" he said.

"I wonder. She doesn't really talk about anyone she used to know on the island. She tells stories about it, but most of them are about wildlife, and harvesting oysters. She goes quiet when I ask about the people."

"She's still alive?" he asked.

"Oh yeah, she's still alive and feisty as ever," Melanie said with a chuckle. "

My grandfather knew every inch of this place. He loved this island. It's sad to see it fading away. Pretty soon it will just be a thing of the past." He paused and looked around, took a deep breath in, exhaled and continued in a low, curious tone, "Have you seen the old gravestones?"

"Gravestones?!" both girls said excitedly in unison.

He led the way to the site of the gravestones, wading through cattails and reeds, their feet leaving foot-sized holes in the sandy marsh behind them. They rounded a hill, and there, tucked in, among the grass were gray, weathered headstones.

He walked up to one with lettering that was still legible.

"This is my favorite one, it's what keeps me coming back to the island," he said, as he wiped the face of an old, faded stone. Then he read the words out loud,

"Effie Lee Wilson
1880-1893
Forget me not, is all I ask, I could not ask for more.
Let them be cherished by my friends so loving and so dear.
Dearest Effie now has left us and our loss we deeply feel.
But tis' God, He has berefted us, He will all our sorrows heal."

The words hung in the air, like a sad, melodic song. A silence fell over them when he finished speaking.

"It's like she knew," Eden said softly, "Like she knew the island was going to fade away, and she was begging not to be forgotten."

"Only 13 years old, how tragic," Melanie said, holding back tears.

"It's something isn't it?" he said. "Pretty soon, all this will be gone. Poor Effie will be gone beneath the bay, and there isn't anything we can do about it."

"There's got to be something someone can do," Eden objected in desperation.

"Nope, the government denied requests to save it,' he said. "My grandpa's friend tried and tried, but there's no stopping it. Pretty soon everything you see here will be returned to the bay."

Wesley 1917

As he rowed farther away from shore and out into the bay, he couldn't help but replay his afternoon spent with Hattie. The thought of her brought a smile to his face, her honesty and bluntness, her girlish features and charm. Her zeal for adventure and life beyond the ordinary was so captivating, so refreshing, he couldn't help but long for more.

A gust of wind blew from the south making it easier to row, so he sat back and let the current carry his boat. He looked out at the water and heard the familiar cry of a blue heron. *The sound is so interesting coming from a bird*, he thought. *Not birdlike at all.*

As he reached old man Tom's dock, the place that he'd come to now call home, he let out a long sigh. He longed for his father and all the memories they had created together. His mother had passed away during his birth, so he never had the chance to meet her. With his father being his sole family, his absence created a profound void in his life. Since his father had passed away, he had felt lost, like a sailboat in the wind, adrift at sea. He was unsure of his direction or destination, with no plan or vision for what was next. But he noticed that this afternoon, something felt different. His time with Hattie had brought something alive in him that had been gone since the loss of his father. She had given him purpose, a new found hope and vision for what could possibly be in the future. It felt good to smile again, to genuinely laugh, to appreciate the company and conversation with another.

He approached the dock and jumped out on it and tied his boat securely to the post of the dock. He grabbed his lunchbox and Hattie's cap and walked towards the small house. As he walked, he couldn't help but dream about the life he could have with her. A house right on the bay, a small garden, kids. He shook his head. *Slow down*, he thought. *You just met her; she probably already has a boyfriend.* Still, he couldn't help but fantasize about a possible future with Hattie.

Gray puffs of smoke rose from the chimney as he reached the place, he now called home. Tom had a fire going and dinner was probably already on the stove, if there was one thing Tom loved, it was dinner time. When Wesley first came to live with Tom, the old man was very quiet most of the day, but at suppertime, he turned into a chatterbox, in between spoonful's of warm seafood he would ramble on and on. Something about a warm dinner in his belly made him happy and personable, welcoming the companionship that Wesley brought. The two would talk and joke in the low glow of the wood stove, eating crab soup and drinking mugs full of dark stouts, staying at the table long after supper was done. This companionship dulled the ache from the loss of Wesley's father.

Wes opened the back door, took off his boots and jacket, and set his lunch box on the counter.

"Dinner is on the stove if you're hungry." Tom said with a spoonful of oyster soup with mixed vegetables tumbling around in his mouth.

"Thank you," Wes replied as he grabbed a bowl from the cupboard and filled it with two large ladles of steaming soup. He filled a glass of water, took his filled bowl, and sat down at the table next to Tom, the old pine chair creaked as he sat into it.

"How was your day?" Tom asked, as he picked up his cup and took a big swig of stout.

"It was pretty great." Wes replied as he scooped up a spoonful of soup.

"Pretty great?!" Tom said in a curious tone. "You don't usually respond with that. Did something happen out of the ordinary?"

Wes tried to conceal a smile.

"Well, I met someone," he said, keeping his eyes fixed on the bowl below him.

"Oh!? I'm guessing this someone was of the opposite sex. Judging by the way you're wanting to grin from ear to ear," Tom said with a cheeky grin. Silence hung between them for a moment. Wes wrestled with wanting to share everything or just keeping his mouth shut, but he felt like Tom had already seen right through him.

"Mhm, and a real pretty one, but she's also different, she isn't all giggly and bashful like the other girls, she says what she's thinking." Wes replied, still refusing to look up, afraid that if he met the old man's eyes, they would reveal disapproval or judgment.

"Oh no, be careful with those kinds, attractive at first, but later they ain't nothing but trouble, spitfire and stubborn as hell," Tom said and shook his pointer finger at Wes playfully.

Wes chuckled at Tom's words.

"I like it when a woman has a mind of her own," Wes said smiling.

"Ha! I don't know about that. An opinionated woman is as dangerous as a storm on the open bay. Captivating, stunningly beautiful, pulling you in, to the point where you're completely in over your head, but you never know what's coming next," Tom said, half joking, half serious.

"Isn't that what makes it interesting, and keeps you on your toes? Have you ever been in love Tom?" Wes questioned.

Tom took a sip of his stout and set his cup down on the table. "I was, once. But that was a long time ago." Tom said, stirring around his stew, his eyes looking away from Wes.

"What happened to her, if you don't mind me asking?" Wes asked.

There was a long pause before Tom spoke, contemplating sharing anything at all.

"My Annie, she had the softest hands, and eyes that were as bright as the blue sky, and she could cook, my goodness she could cook," the old man said with a smile that was both happy and sad, his memories flooding the forefront of his mind. "We had a daughter together; she was like a sunburst. Wild and happy, she always begged to come fishing with me, she was the joy of our lives." Tom took a deep breath and continued, "She was thirteen years old when she got real sick, a bad fever, and no one could help her. She passed away," Tom said low. He took a long breath and then continued. "The death of our daughter was too much for my wife, she couldn't bear the loss of her. I found her face down in the bay a month after our daughter died." Tom picked up his cup and took another drink. A silence fell over them, the fire crackled in the background, shadows and light flickered and danced against the wall and ceiling.

"I'm so sorry Tom," Wes said in almost a whisper.

"They are buried in the family plot, not too far from here, my Annie, and our daughter, Effie Lee."

Tom took a sip from his cup and sat back in chair, crossed his arms over his chest and stared at the ceiling, moments passed in silence, Tom cleared his throat, and began to speak. "Here's what I can tell you young man, if you're brave enough to give your heart away, and lucky enough to receive love in return, take hold of it with two hands and never let it go. It's the only thing in life worth living and dying for."

Chapter Six

Hattie 1917

Dinner was on the table by the time Hattie and her father put the oysters away and cleaned up. Ollie and her mother were seated and waiting for them to come in and take a seat.

"Happy birthday Hattie!" her mother said as they walked in the back door. "I made your favorite dessert, coconut cream pie!"

Hattie smiled as she slipped off her boots.

"Thank you, Mama," Hattie said with a smile as she and her father sat down at the table.

"The Banks, Rogers and the Stewarts are leaving for the mainland," Ollie exclaimed with a mouth full of food.

"Don't talk with your mouth full," his mother scolded him.

"Who told you that?!" Hattie asked. "My teacher told us today at the end of class." The room fell silent.

"That means there are only a handful of us left," Amelia said in a low tone.

"Will we be next?" Ollie asked, wiping his mouth.

"No. This is our home," Henry said sternly. No one said anything else during the rest of dinner.

Towards the end of dinner, Hattie's mother got up from her seat and pulled the pie from the fridge. She sliced generous-sized pieces and placed them on everyone's plate.

"Yum!" Ollie exclaimed with his eyes wide and his mouth salivating, as he quickly picked up his fork and dove into his piece, shoveling large bites into his mouth.

"Ollie, slow down! You'll get a tummy ache," his mother scolded him.

Hattie smiled at her brother, thinking about how lucky he was to be young and carefree, wishing she could go back to those days when life was simple, going to school with friends, playing hopscotch and riding bikes, blissfully unaware of the world and the changes going on around them.

In April, the United States declared war on Germany. Many of the boys Hattie grew up with were now contemplating serving their country, talking about it like it was a fun vacation or a game that people played for fun. She had seen the vibrant, enticing posters around town, glamorizing war, and advertising heroism. Hattie knew little about war and couldn't understand why anyone would willingly sign up to put their life on the line or worse, take the life of another man.

Hattie's mother placed a present wrapped in brown crate paper and tied with a big satin yellow bow on the table in front of her.

"Happy birthday dear, I hope you like it," her mother said sweetly as she kissed the top of Hattie's head and then sat back down in her seat. Hattie untied the ribbon and tore open the paper. She held up a simple, pale blue cotton dress with a cream collar and a cream sweater.

"They're lovely, thank you," Hattie said, trying her best to sound excited. *Why did her mother always insist on buying her such plain and boring clothes? If she was going to spend money on new clothes, why not buy something with a little more flair?* she thought. She gave an appreciative smile as she folded and set the pieces back on the wrapping paper. She picked up her plate and cup and took them to the sink.

"No, no, birthday girl. You don't have to do dishes tonight. Ollie will handle that." Her father said with a smile as he patted Ollie on the shoulder, Ollie grunted and slumped his shoulders.

"Would you be a dear and try them on Hattie?" Her mother asked, her hands gently clapping.

"Sure." Hattie said as she took a deep breath. The last thing she wanted to do was put on a plain dress and sweater and force a twirl in front of her family. What she really wanted was to take a long hot bath and go to bed. But she knew her mother would be upset and give her a guilt trip if she didn't oblige. She picked the dress and sweater off the table and went upstairs to change in her room. A few moments later she returned downstairs in the plain blue dress that hung loosely around her figure with the cream cardigan on top that would've fit just about as well as a potato sack.

"Oh Hattie, you look beautiful. That color really brings out your eyes." Her mother said with a smile as she adjusted the sweater that hung like a towel on her shoulders. "Isn't she lovely?" Amelia asked, glancing at Henry, who was now seated in his favorite chair by a crackling fire reading today's newspaper.

He looked up, his eyes looking over the rim of his reading glasses.

"Mhm" he agreed and glanced back down at the paper. Amelia patted Hattie on the back and then headed into the kitchen to help Ollie finish the dishes.

Hattie walked over and slumped down on the couch next to her father's chair by the fire. She stared at the warm colors dancing against the black logs, the mesmerizing flicker put her in a daze and for some reason, Wesley came to her mind at that moment. His face, his strong jawline, and the colors of his stubble that speckled across his cheeks and chin, the reds, and blondes mixed with dark browns, the way his eyes came alive with their own fire whenever he looked at her. She let her mind wander with the ideas of what it would be like to kiss him, touch him, allow him to touch her. Her heart raced and her stomach fluttered at the thought.

"Something on your mind kiddo?" her father asked, with the newspaper still in front of his face. She suddenly jolted back to reality, her gaze shifting away from the crackling fire, as if she was ashamed that her father could have glimpsed into her thoughts. She cleared her throat.

"No, just thinking." Hattie replied as she tapped her foot nervously on the floor.

Her father put down the newspaper and looked at her. He smiled with a little bit of sadness, realizing that she was no longer a little girl, but now a young woman. He realized that she would probably soon leave their home to start a life of her own.

"You are growing up so fast," he said. "I'm sorry we couldn't send you to a university in the city. I know how much you've wanted to go," he said as he reached out for her hand and gave it a quick squeeze.

"It's alright, I understand," Hattie replied with a bashful smile. "Besides, who would help you if I went?" she said half joking but half serious.

"That's a good point," he said with a small chuckle. "But you deserve to see the world, I know how much you want to get off this island."

Hattie gazed at him, her eyes welling up with tears. His unexpected words caught her completely off guard. He had always been a reserved, quiet man.

Their conversations usually revolved around the ever-changing weather, the abundance of oysters, the bay, or how to successfully catch and clean fish.

"Thank you, Pa," she said, swallowing back tears. He reached into his pocket, reached for her hand, and put a $5 bill in her palm.

"Happy birthday my girl, don't give up on your dreams."

Hattie looked down in her hand, saw the bill and gasped.

"Oh my! Pa, this is too much! I can't take this." He held up a hand to silence her.

"That's yours, keep it. Besides, you brought in quite a haul today," he said with a smile and picked his newspaper back up and continued reading. Hattie smiled, stood to her feet and kissed him on the top of his head.

"Goodnight Pa," she said with a smile as she made her way up the stairs, holding the bill in her hand.

Chapter Seven

Wesley 1917

Wesley was up before dawn the rest of the week, harvesting as many oysters as he could, and when he'd harvested the max amount allowed, he went fishing. He was on a mission to save up enough money to take Hattie to Greene's opera house in Cambridge Maryland. After their chance encounter on the bay, he felt an unwavering determination to see her again and do something meaningful for her. He had heard of the live, provocative, jazz music and risky dancing that went on at Greene's on Saturday nights, and he wanted to take her and sweep her off her feet. He had seen the excitement and longing in Hattie's eyes as she talked about her dreams of leaving the island, and he wanted to be the one to make that happen for her. He'd known girls on Smith Island but most of them seemed superficial and materialistic, caring only about the latest hairstyle and fashion but little about anything with real meaning or depth. But his conversation with Hattie had been completely different. He was captivated by Hattie's authenticity. She didn't try to impress him with rehearsed or forced responses. Her answers were unfiltered and blunt, and he found that incredibly refreshing.

Weeks had passed since they had first met, he had harvested as much as he could and went up north to sell his catch for a bigger profit. Up north they revered the Maryland Chesapeake Bay Oysters as a delicacy and paid twice as much for them. Wes made multiple trips and slept very little over the past weeks, spending long days out on the water. But he'd finally saved up a good bit of money, enough for dinner and an evening at Greene's. He had visited Cambridge last week to see if he could get tickets to see the jazz band that was playing next weekend. Posters were plastered all over Cambridge promoting the up-and-coming jazz band that had gained national attention. Luckily, there were still a few tickets available; he had scored seats to the Dixieland Jazz band, five-piece jazz band from Louisiana. He had no idea who they were but everyone in town seemed to know.

He woke up early in the morning; the sun was just beginning to make its appearance for the day. Autumn had been surprisingly mild this year, summer's warmth held on until the last days of October. He sprung out of bed, today would be the day that he would find Hattie and reveal his plan to take her to Cambridge.

His stomach somersaulted at the thought of seeing her again; doubt crept in at the corners of his mind, and he started to second-guess his decision. *What if she refused? What if she was insulted by his gesture? What if she thought he was being too forward? After all, she had called him crazy, but wasn't it playfully?* He now found himself questioning everything about their first conversation, trying to recall her tone and facial expressions when they talked. His fingers fumbled as he buttoned up his shirt, his hands shook as he smoothed the hair that stuck up on the top of his head. He tried to push the thoughts to the back of his mind while he finished getting dressed and made his way to the kitchen, taking deep breaths and exhaling loudly to try and calm his nerves. He buttered a day-old biscuit and opened a jar of canned peaches and forked a few into his mouth. Old man Tom had brought a few jars home from church this past summer. The ladies at the church always made sure to check in on him and gave him plenty of goodies to keep his belly full. Wes grabbed his metal lunch pail and put two pieces of bread, some cheese and some lumps of crab meat inside it, hoping to relive their first lunch together. He took a thermos of coffee and a bottle of sweet red table wine that he picked up while he was in Cambridge. He didn't know if Hattie had ever drank wine before, but he thought it might be fun to have a cup with her as they ate lunch together. He put two mugs in a canvas sack along with the bottle of wine, and her wool cap that she had left in his boat. He slid on his boots and jacket and quickly went out the back door that slapped against its wooden frame behind him.

Tom was in the shed gathering nets and rakes, his round face looked up when heard the screen door slam.

"Up early again?" he hollered.

"Yes sir, got some things I need to do today," he said with a boyish grin.

"I see, well good luck to ya," Tom said as he held up a net that he was mending.

"Thank you, I'll see you later for supper," he called to him over his shoulder as he made his way to the dock.

The sun was in full display now, casting bright gold and warm amber across the sky, causing the bay's ripples to shimmer with its reflection. Wes stopped for a moment and took it all in, "absolutely stunning," he thought to himself. Why anyone would ever want to leave this place was beyond him. He loaded up his boat and set off to find his oyster girl.

Chapter Eight

Hattie 1917

The golden rays of the morning sunshine shone through her window, gently kissing her face as she awoke. Her father would be gone for a few days selling oysters to buyers up north. Customers were paying twice the price in New York that they were going for in Maryland and her father wanted to take advantage of the opportunity to double his profits. She begged him to take her with him, but he argued that it was no place for a young lady. She pleaded with her mother to talk to him and convince him to take her, but she just shook her head and said, "If your father said no, then it's a no." Hattie would be on her own again today harvesting oysters by hand in the now frigid water.

She had quite a bit of money saved up and was hopeful that she would be able to have enough to go see a jazz band by the spring of next year. She slid out from under her cozy, warm blankets reluctantly, got dressed and tied her hair into a braid that fell down the center of her back. Small, childlike curls fell around her forehead, she tried to smooth them out with her spit and fingers, but they quickly rebelled and bounced back to their former state, curly and wild. She could smell cheesy grits and bacon cooking in the kitchen and her stomach rumbled in anticipation.

Ollie was in his usual spot at the table, a bowl full of steaming grits in front of him. He was reading the headlines of today's newspaper, another headline about the war. She picked up a spoonful of the warm grits from his bowl and took a bite.

"Hey! Hattie!" Ollie whined, as he grabbed his spoon out of her hand. She swallowed and smiled at him. He grunted in annoyance.

"You shouldn't be reading this," Hattie said as she picked up the newspaper and briefly skimmed the headlines.

"I'm old enough," he protested.

"Hardly," she said as she set it back down.

"I wonder if they'll still be at war when I'm 18?" he asked, as he put a full spoonful of grits in his mouth.

"I don't know, I sure hope not," Hattie replied as she walked over to the stove and filled a bowl with grits, she took a piece of bacon and crumbled it on top.

"Well, if they are, I'm going to be a soldier and fight in the war," Ollie said with confidence as he scooped up another full spoon of grits and put it in his mouth.

Hattie spun around in a fury to face her brother, dropping her spoon loudly against her bowl. "No, you will absolutely not!" she scolded, "are you trying to get yourself killed? I don't understand boys and the desire to go kill someone or get killed themselves!" She said as she picked up her spoon and flung it towards the air, pieces of grits flew towards the ceiling.

"Well, I'll be a man and I'll make my own choices, and no one will be able to tell me what to do," he said, staring into his grits, his brow furrowed and serious, he picked up another spoonful and put it in his mouth.

"What in heaven's name is going on in here?" Their mother asked as she came in from the living room holding a pair of their father's pants she was mending.

"Oh nothing, Ollie just wants to go get himself killed in the war when he's 18, that's all," Hattie said sarcastically as she sat down at the table and began eating her breakfast.

"Oh for heaven's sake, that's enough!" Amelia replied as she picked up the newspaper and tucked it under her armpit.

"It's alright momma, I'll be a man, and I'll make you and papa real proud," Ollie said as he looked at her with his chest puffed up.

"Oh my sweet boy," their mother said as she squatted down to be eye level with him. "You are brave, and we are already so very proud of you." She said as she brushed her hand on his cheekbone and continued "I would be so very sad if you left. But I know you will make your own choices; I just hope and pray that you make the best ones for you and no one else." He smiled and stared at her. "But let's not talk about this now, you have plenty of time to decide, finish up your breakfast and get to school." She said as she stood up. "Hattie don't forget to take something to eat for lunch today." their mother said as she walked to Hattie and kissed the top of her head. "Now, no more fighting, I've got to finish these pants before your father comes home," she said as she walked out of the kitchen and back into the living room.

Hattie took the last bite of her grits and placed her bowl in the sink. She didn't like the thought of her little brother dreaming of going to war, but he was right. If that was something he wanted to do when he was older, there was nothing anyone could do about it.

She sighed and turned towards him, "have a good day, Ollie." she said, tousling his hair as she walked towards the back door and grabbed her coat.

Where in the world did I put my cap? she thought, as she slid on her boots and headed out the door. She made her way across the yard, passed the little garden, dried up vegetable plants clinging to the fence, brown and dead. The wooden door on the shed creaked as she flew it open, the hinges eaten with rust from the salty bay water. She glanced around the small wooden shed. It held the same familiar smell of pine, dirt, and tin. She used to play here as a child, she would stack the crates and build a castle and pretend to be a queen who ruled the land. Her father would scold her and tell her it was too dangerous and that she would hurt herself on the old, splintered crates, but she kept doing it anyway, making sure she put the crates back when she was done playing. She grabbed a stack of crates, the rake and walked to the shoreline. Despite the cold air, the bay seemed alive this morning. Gulls flew all around, teasing and taunting each other, a turtle made a splash as it jumped into the cold water. Pelicans sat and stretched out their wings on the posts of the dock in the distance. They reminded her of Wes, and how he told her why they turned their heads before diving into the water.

It had been weeks since their first meeting on the bay. Had he forgotten about her? Had their chance encounter been nothing more than a coincidence? Had he moved on that quick? He was probably wooing some other girl on the island with his charm and sweet-talking words. She had made a joke about him being a smooth talker when they first met, but she didn't want to believe that it was true.

There had been boys Hattie had known over the years that had been flirty with her when she was in school, but they had all seemed to do it for sport, flirting with every girl in class just to see which one would play along and flirt back. Hattie would roll her eyes and think how pathetic it was when the other girls would giggle, blush coloring on their cheeks. They would twirl their hair when the boys would simply say "hey beautiful!" as they rode by on their bikes after school. *Don't they realize that they say it to every girl!?* she would think as she walked on, ignoring their cat calls.

But Wesley's words and compliments seemed different. They seemed genuine. Something about the way he stared at her. He stared into her eyes and cutting through to her soul. His smile, like it was a privilege just to be with her. The way he talked with honesty and ease had made her believe him, and even though she didn't want to admit it, she really wanted to see him again. *But I guess I was wrong*, she thought as she brought the rake high above her head and plunged it into the shallow, murky water.

Eden 1982

Eden and Melanie spent the day exploring the island with the boy, trudging through tall grasses, climbing over small hills, walking along sandy shorelines and rocky beaches. Seeing all kinds of wildlife and discovering little treasures from the past. Broken dishes, glass bottles, old, stamped bricks, a medicine tin, an empty turtle shell, a few shark teeth, and some oyster shells. The boy told all the stories he had heard from his grandfather and impressed them with his knowledge of the wildlife on the island.

"Did you know that herons are thought to have communicated with the gods?" he said after a large heron flew over them, its wings cast a shadow on their faces. Seagulls squawked and cawed on the shoreline, fighting over an insect. "And gulls stamp their feet in a group to imitate rainfall, tricking the worms to come to the surface." He said as they watched the swarm of the chatty, energetic birds.

"No way!" Eden said with a chuckle, "I always thought they were silly birds that weren't very smart. Guess not!" They walked to the shoreline and picked out a sandy spot to sit and eat lunch, sharing what they had brought with the boy.

"So where do you live?" Melanie asked him bluntly as she took a large bite of her sandwich.

"Crisfield, Maryland, just north of here on the eastern shore," he replied, as he took a swig of a soda. "What about you two?" he asked.

"We live in Ridge Maryland, about an hour from here across the bay," Eden replied.

"Wow! And y'all managed to get here on your own?! Impressive," he said with a small chuckle.

"We're actually very smart." Melanie snapped back, "I bet you probably wouldn't even be able to do it, you'd end up lost somewhere out in the bay." she said as she motioned her hand towards the water.

"Jeez Melanie, chill!" Eden replied with a laugh. "How often do you come here?" Eden asked.

"Not as much as I used to," He replied. "It's not as much fun when you come by yourself." Eden shook her head in understanding. "I mostly come to see how much is left. They say it will be completely underwater within the next 20 years, give or take." He paused and looked around, taking it all in. "I can't imagine it, all of it just, disappearing." His words were carried off, swept by the wind and flew over and through the tall grasses and landscape, as though the island felt the gravity and depth of its impending extinction. The girls looked around at all that surrounded them, trying to imagine it all gone, trying to imagine only bay water covering the island and taking with it all its history and stories, burying them in a watery grave. This island was part of her history, part of who she was, she was a direct descendant from this island, and it felt like she wasn't just losing a piece of land she was also losing a piece of her. Eden had a sinking thought that someday boaters would be passing right over it without any idea it was ever there at all.

"Well, we better be heading back, it's getting late," Melanie said nonchalantly, unaware of the effect the boy's words were having on Eden. Melanie stood and knocked the sand off the bottom of her shorts.

Eden jumped up, "Oh, my gosh! What time is it?" she asked.

The boy pulled out an old, bronze pocket watch from the pocket of his shorts and flipped it open. "It's 4:15 pm," He answered as he closed it and slid it back in his pocket. The girls stared at him.

"What in the world?" Melanie said. "Who carries around an old watch like that?" she said with a chuckle. Eden couldn't help but laugh at Melanie's bluntness.

The boy looked at them, not surprised by their response to his watch. "It was my grandfather's. He gave it to me right before I lost him, he always carried it with him." He said with a small grin, remembering the way his grandfather pulled it out of his pocket every now and then to check the time.

"Oh, I'm sorry, I didn't..." Melanie's words trailed off, not sure what to say. "It's fine," he replied, "I know, there aren't many kids my age carrying around antique pocket watches." He said with a chuckle.

"It's really cool." Eden said, "Can I look at it?" she asked.

"Sure," he said as he pulled it from his pocket and handed it to her. The front of it had an open scroll-faced, hinged cover with intricate scroll patterns, she flipped it over. The back had a raised seagull that flew over a shoreline. She ran her finger over the detail of the bird, feeling its bumps and lines. She held it up to her face to examine it more closely.

"It's beautiful," she said as she slowly handed it back to him.

"Thanks," he replied, as he slid it back in his pocket.

The three of them made their way back to the boats that were still where they left them at the other end of the island.

"You two go ahead and get in, I'll push you off," the boy said.

"What about you?" Eden asked.

"I can push myself out and jump in the side, I've done it many times." he said confidently.

"Alright," Melanie said quickly as threw her empty lunch bag over the side of the boat and climbed in.

Eden turned to the boy, "Thank you, and thanks for showing us around the island, it really is a beautiful place," she said smiling.

"My pleasure," he responded.

"I'd love to do it again sometime." She said in a shy but sweet tone.

"Me too! Come back next week? Same time?" he asked.

"I can try," she said with a smile.

"Eden, come on! We're going to be late!" Melanie hollered from the boat.

Eden furrowed her brows and looked at Melanie, "I'm coming!" She said annoyed.

"Better get going," he said with a smile. Eden climbed in the boat and took her seat. The boy put his hands on the front of the boat, leaned forward and shoved it into the water behind them with all his strength. Melanie started up the engine and slowly moved the boat forward.

Eden looked at the boy as he started to get farther and farther away, then realized she never asked him his name. She called out, "What's your name?!"

"Hudson!" he yelled back, as he slowly faded into the distant shoreline and disappeared into the blue horizon.

Wesley 1917

He came around the corner of the south side of the island and saw her. His breath caught in his chest. She was in the same spot as she was when he first saw her that first October morning, throwing a stone at the seagulls. He smiled and chuckled to himself at the memory of it; her face when she had slipped and fallen, the wet strands of hair that hung down the front of her forehead, the way she looked at him, her face furious. He couldn't help but think how adorable she looked at that moment. He had hoped he would see her again but wasn't sure she would still be here. She seemed so determined to get off the island and start a new exciting life on the mainland.

Holland Island was a small town, but their paths had never crossed before, they never saw each other in town or on the water. Wes kept to himself most of the time, if he or Tom needed anything from town

Tom was the one who went to get it. Tom loved trips to town, his guilty pleasure was gossip and Betty, the choir director, was always happy to share it. Betty spread gossip faster than wildfire in a dead hayfield. Wes stayed away from people like that. *You can't trust 'em,* he thought.

He rowed closer to her, his stomach was doing summersaults, his heart felt like it was going to beat outside of his chest. Her figure grew closer and closer with every row, he couldn't wait to see her face again, stare into her ocean-blue eyes, and tell her about the gift he had for her.

As he grew closer Hattie was still unaware of his presence. He didn't want to scare her again, so he called to her, "Hello oyster girl."

Her back was to him. She froze, pulled the rake close to her body, and slowly turned her head in his direction. She squinted and then realized who it was, and a big smile took over her face. She quickly tried to get rid of her smile, not wanting him to see how glad she was to see him, but the corners of her lips lingered upward.

"Hello Wes," she said, trying to sound as if she weren't amused to see him. He was beside her now in his boat, the side of it bumped up against her leg. "You trying to run me over?" she teased.

"No," he chuckled as he leaned over to hold onto her rake to keep from hitting her again. "Could you pull me in?" he asked.

She looked at him curiously.

"Why should I? I am very busy at the moment," she said, her smile taking over her face. He could tell she was trying to play hard to get but failing miserably.

He leaned in; his nose just inches from her nose, his eyes stared intently into hers.

"Because I have something for you that I think you'll love," he said in almost a whisper, without blinking.

"Oh really?!" she questioned, her eyes staring back into his, her knees felt weak, feeling very uneasy at how close they were, but his eyes were too intense to look away and she really liked this playful back and forth.

"Mhm," he said, their noses still almost touching. They lingered there for a moment, their eyes staring, the air between them suspenseful and thin. She pulled back, grabbed the front of his boat and walked it to the shoreline. He jumped out and helped her pull the boat onto the beach. He took the rake from her hand and set it over by her crates.

"Have you eaten lunch yet?" he asked as he walked back to her.

"No, I forgot to bring lunch with me," she said, looking down at the sand, her foot nervously nudged at a broken seashell. He reached his hand to her face and lifted her chin.

"Well good thing I brought plenty then," he said with a smile. He walked past her and climbed into the boat that was mostly on the beach now. "Come have lunch with me, Oyster girl," he said as he patted the seat next to him. She smiled and hesitated for a moment, then shrugged her shoulders and climbed into the boat and took the seat beside him. She watched as he unpacked the lunch he had prepared for them.

Clearly, he had planned this, she thought. She didn't know whether to be flattered or concerned. Weeks had gone by, and she hadn't seen or heard from him, so why is he being so thoughtful now?

"So, you get tired of all the other girls?" she asked half-jokingly, half-accusingly.

He stopped and stared at her in confusion, "other girls?!" he asked with his brows furrowed, "I don't know what you're talking about."

"Right," she said sarcastically and crossed her arms, "then why have you been gone so long? Isn't that why you haven't come back to see me?" She questioned.

His eyes full of confusion and worry, "Hattie, I have been working from dawn until sundown, saving up money." He said as he reached for his bag and pulled out the tickets for the jazz band, "for these." He held them out to her, she stared at the tickets, her eyes grew wider as she realized what they were, she darted her eyes back at him. "They're for…" his voice paused before he said the next word, "Us, this Saturday, if you want to go?" His eyes searched her face for a response. She sat, frozen, her eyes looking back at the tickets, her eyes brimming with tears. She reached for them, taking them from his hand, reading them over and over. "Well?" He questioned, "what do you say?" The air hung between them; she hadn't looked up at him in minutes. His stomach dropped, he braced himself for the rejection that he was sure to follow.

"Wes," she said in almost a whisper, "I can't accept these, it's too much."

"Nonsense!" he replied, "I know how much you've wanted to go, and I wanted to be the one to take you. But if you don't want to go with me, I understand, take whoever you want-"

"I want to!" she said cutting him off, she looked up at him, and smiled with tears in her eyes. Wes' breath caught in his throat, she was so beautiful, so pure. "Yes, I want to go with you. This is the nicest, most thoughtful thing anyone has ever done for me. I can't believe you got these!" she said, looking back at the tickets in her hand. Wes reached out and wiped at the tears that trickled down her cheeks. "You're going to have to ask my Pa if I can go," she said with a little smile.

"I already did," He replied with a grin.

"WHAT?" she said, shocked and curious.

"Yep, I saw him in town the other day with your mother at the general store. He was carrying a 5lb bag of flour home for her. I knew it was your folks because your mother looks a lot like you, same dimple when you smile. I figured that was my chance to get their permission." Wes said, smiling that he was able to surprise her, enjoying this moment a little too much.

"They knew, and never said anything!?" she exclaimed, her voice holding surprise and emotion.

"They love you, and they know how much you want to see something other than this island," he said, "They checked with old man Tom and asked about my character," he continued slightly chuckling.

"Oh heavens," Hattie said as she covered her face with her hands, slightly embarrassed by her parents' behavior. "Well, I guess I have to go with you now, now that my parents know, and gave you their approval," Hattie said sarcastically. Wes laughed at her response.

"Well, I guess so!" he said with a low chuckle.

Chapter Eleven

Hattie 1917

It felt like Saturday would never come. Hattie barely slept the night before, her mind restless and wandering. Every time she closed her eyes to sleep, images would flood her thoughts. Her and Wesley in downtown Cambridge, having dinner, talking, dancing.

If you could just fall asleep the day will be here! she thought, annoyed with herself. She already had her outfit for the day layer on a wooden chair in the corner of her bedroom. Her light blue cotton dress and cardigan that her parents gave her for her birthday, and her worn, brown pair of shoes with a single brass button on each sat on the floor below. Her parents were surprisingly supportive of the outing, her mother more so than her father.

"I would like to meet him again and have a few words before you two go," he had told her sternly when they agreed that she could go, her mother stood next to her father and gave her a little smile.

Hattie opened her eyes, the sun was trying to pierce through her foggy window, it was Saturday morning. She rubbed her eyes and sat up. Wesley told her he'd be there to pick her up around 2 pm, this gave her enough time to help shuck the oysters from yesterday's haul with her brother and father and get cleaned up and dressed, but she'd need to get moving.

There was a low knock on her door, it slowly creaked open, as her mother walked in. "Good morning!" She said with a smile, in her hands, she held a brown paper sack tied with jute string. She set it down on Hattie's lap, "for you, for today's big date," she said, the smile still on her face.

Hattie looked sleepily at the package then at her mother, the sleepy sand still clinging to the corners of her eyes. Hattie untied the string and opened the ends of the paper to reveal a tunic style dress, with a light pink liner and a cream lace overlay, with a pink satin ribbon wrapped around it at the waistline. Under the dress sat a pair of cream-colored pumps with a low heel and pearl buttons that clasped at the strap. Hattie held up the dress, her eyes trying to take it in, trying to comprehend that this was really hers.

Her mouth fell open as she touched the lace and trailed her finger over the pink satin ribbon. "It's the prettiest thing I've ever seen." She said in a whisper. "Thank you so much!" She dropped the dress in her lap and leaped to her mother, wrapping her arms around her neck, tears brimming in her eyes. *Maybe her mother's sense of style wasn't so bad after all,* she thought.

"You really like it?" her mother asked.

"Like it? I love it!" Hattie exclaimed, wiping the tears that had spilled out of her eyes and rolled down her cheeks. Her mother held Hattie's face in her hands and looked into her eyes.

"You deserve this, my beautiful girl," Hattie's mother said, her own eyes filled with tears. At that moment Hattie saw the same look in her mother's eyes that she recognized in her own: adventure and excitement. She had never thought of her mother as having dreams and ambitions of her own.

What was she like when she was young? Hattie thought. She had never asked her mother about her life as a young girl. She had always seen her as an older woman who was plain and boring, stuck in the routines of a monotonous, housewife role, someone Hattie never wanted to be. But here, sitting on her bed, she saw similarities of herself in her mother. Hattie let herself imagine her mother as a young, free-spirited, woman staring back at her. And for a brief moment, she wondered if her mother ever wished for a different life, if she had ever daydreamed of what a life off of the island might have looked like.

It took just over 4 hours to get the oysters cleaned and shucked. It was now 1:15 pm. Hattie's father told her to go get cleaned up and that he and her brother could finish cleaning up the leftover oyster shells and tools. Hattie ran across the backyard, flew open the back door and quickly made her way through the kitchen and up the stairs to the washroom. She kicked her muddy boots off, sending them flying across the room, hitting the wall and then landing on the floor with a loud thump. She quickly undressed, and dropped her smelly, damp clothes to the floor. Raw, fishy smelling oysters was the last thing she wanted to smell like on her date, even though that's what Wes had always called her…Oyster girl.

She found the pet name annoying and somewhat insulting at first, but now it had grown on her. Hattie had noticed that there was a change in the way he said it now. There was affection behind the words, the way the corners of his mouth would curl slightly, revealing a flirty little grin. His eyes twinkled with the excitement of attraction, and then would quickly dart them towards the ground, trying to avoid eye contact, knowing that if she looked in, she would see right through him.

The truth was, she was falling for him just as hard and fast as he was falling for her. She didn't understand or recognize herself now. Who was this young woman who got butterflies in the pit of her stomach when her fingers would barely brush against his? Who was this young woman who would scan the horizon of the bay, looking for his boat out among the others, hoping to get a glance of his silhouette against the backdrop of the darkened gray sky? She would even catch herself dreaming more about a life with Wes than a life in the city. She felt her heartstrings being tugged and slowly opening to the idea of love and marriage. Something she usually gave very little thought or desire to, she had always wanted to be independent, secure, a free spirit that didn't need to depend on a man for her security and sense of belonging. But maybe you could have both. Maybe you could still be a free spirit and have love with another. Maybe being in love didn't mean being weak, maybe it made you stronger. Maybe you could give yourself away but gain another in return. Maybe love meant that someone came alongside you and saddled your hopes and dreams, encouraged you to achieve all the things you wanted in life. What was it about this boy that had brought such a shift inside her? Her mind wondered about these questions and the newfound desires that had taken hold in her as she washed her hair and body and then drained the dirty water from the washtub, all the while taking long deep breaths, trying to settle the nerves that were rattling around and clawing at her insides.

The town of Cambridge was unlike anything Hattie had ever seen before. So many people, shops, and restaurants up and down every street, a busy, but wonderful buzz filled every space around them. The air was filled with delightful aromas of freshly baked goods and steaming pots brimming with a variety of the day's fresh catches, wafting through the air, enticing the senses. Shop owners hollered out their sales, the clip-clopping of shoes on the cobblestone streets of shoppers passing by. For a moment the two of them just stood in the middle of the street and took it all in. A car horn called out and the two of them jumped and moved out of the way, laughing.

Hattie turned to Wesley with her eyes full of excitement and wonder. "Where should we go first?" Her face gave way to a wide smile.

Wes simply smiled at her, taking her in, "Wherever you want." He said as he brushed a lock of hair that had escaped from the bun at the back of her neck. She paused, her eyes darting to her feet, unsure how to react to his touch. He lifted her chin, looked into her eyes, and said, "This is your night, and you get to choose."

Hattie couldn't help but blush. She lifted her hand to his and squeezed it in excitement.

"Let's go find something to eat," she said with a smile as she began to pull him along the street.

They had roasted duck and steamed clams for dinner, it was the most delicious thing Hattie had ever tasted. Time flew by as they talked and laughed and shared stories of childhood and similarities and differences of life growing up on the island.

"We'd better get going if we want to get to Greene's in time for the show," Wes said softly. They paid for the meal and hurried to Greene's; they could hear the lively music that was just beginning to play. The room was dark and seductive, dimly lit lamps aligned the walls adorned with crystals that seemed to dance and sparkle with the music. Velvet couches and chairs were placed around the room, people sat with cigarettes pinched between their fingers in one hand, and cocktails in the other. The stage was at the back of the room. Deep mahogany wood covered the face of it, outlined in scrolled trim. The five-piece band used every inch of the stage, the trombone, trumpet, and clarinet players moved around in a sporadic synchronized dance. Women swayed in their beaded, fringed dresses; men tapped along to the jazzy, provocative sounds. The saxophone danced through the air cutting through all the other sounds. It was unlike anything Hattie had ever witnessed, she felt it deep in her chest and fingers.

Wes wrapped his arms around her as they swayed and danced to the music, both unsure of how to dance to such music. The two of them twirled around, clumsily holding each other and laughing nervously when Hattie's toes accidentally got stepped on. But, slowly with each new song they got better and more relaxed and more comfortable. Their bodies got closer, their eyes finding each other and staying locked onto one another. Shallow breaths rose and fell as their mouths grew closer. Wes looked longingly at Hattie's full, youthful lips, desperately wanting to taste them.

Hattie caught his eyes staring at her mouth. She took a shallow breath and leaned in. Their mouths met in nervous desire, their lips giving into the prolonged passion they had bottled up. Slowly they pulled back and just stared at each other as the music swirled up and around them. Then just as quickly as the show started, it was over. Applause and cheers rose from all around and the two of them snapped back into reality.

Breaking their gaze, they made their way from Greene's and headed towards the dock where Wes' boat was tied and waiting to take them home, their hands and fingers still interlocked with each other.

Hattie stopped at a street vendor who was selling pocket watches and trinkets. Each one was a work of art.

"Look at these!" Hattie said in admiration. "Look how beautiful they are." She picked up a pocket watch that had a carving of seagulls flying over the ocean. "I'll take this one please." She handed the man the $5 that her father had given her. The shop owner gave her the change and smiled. She put the change and the pocket watch in her purse and the two of them walked to the boat and sailed by lantern light back to Holland Island.

Chapter Twelve

Eden 1982

Eden and Melanie clambered out of the boat and quickly made their way back to Eden's house. As they got closer Eden could hear chatter and music coming from her backyard. Her friends and family were gathering to celebrate her birthday. She couldn't help but smile thinking about all her friends and family who would surround her to celebrate her turning into an adult, but for some reason, she couldn't shake the thought of Hudson from her mind. She couldn't wait to find her grandmother to tell her all about the things she had seen and discovered on the island. She also wanted to ask her about some of the things Hudson had told her. She wished she would've asked him his last name, maybe her grandmother knew his grandfather, or maybe they lived there at the same time.

"You ok?" Melanie asked.

Eden snapped out of her daze.

"Yeah, I'm fine."

"Well hurry up and let's get to your party, every-one's waiting and you're just standing there!" Melanie said with a smile.

The two girls headed to the backyard, everyone yelled "Happy Birthday!" when they came into view.

Eden smiled and said "Thanks!" There were bal-loons tied to a large picnic table with BBQ chicken, pasta salad, potato salad, watermelon, and cupcakes. A large cooler sat on the ground filled with ice, beer, and soda.

Eden's mom came over to her with an open beer,

"Here you go baby girl, happy birthday," she said as she handed her the beer and kissed her on the cheek. "I'll let you have a few, but only because it's your birthday."

"Thanks, mom," Eden replied, taking the beer and giving it a long swig. "Where's grandma?" Eden asked as she looked around the yard.

"She's inside, she was out here earlier but it got a little too hot for her." Eden set her beer on the table, said hello to a few friends and then made her way through the back porch to the small kitchen.

It was plain and simple with its blue and white gingham curtains and creamy yellow paint, white cab-inets, and butcher block countertops. Somehow the small room always felt warm, and welcoming, the smell of coffee and bread always lingered in the air. Her grandmother was sitting at the small table with a glass of lemonade, staring blankly out the window that faced the backyard.

"Hey Grandma," Eden said, pulling her out of her trance.

"Hey birthday girl!" her grandmother said with a sweet smile. Eden sat down in the chair beside her. Her grandmother reached over and put her soft, wrinkled hand to Eden's cheek. "How did you get to be so grown up?" Her grandmother asked.

Eden smiled and looked down, her cheeks flushing slightly.

"I don't know, time flies I guess," Eden said with a little chuckle.

"Yes, it does, time flies. It takes off and carries the years away, and then. Before you know it, you're left staring at the back end of it, asking where it's going and you're calling for it to come back." Her grandmother's voice was soft and low.

Eden stared at her; her eyes seemed to hide so much that Eden didn't know, so much about her life that she had never talked to her about. Eden wanted to know, she wanted to ask so many questions, but she wasn't sure how her grandmother would respond. Would she get upset and shut down? The last thing she wanted to do was make her upset, but she was so curious about her life growing up on the island, the island that she had just walked and explored. Walking on what was left of it had felt like it was a part of her, like there were ties and pulls linking her to its ground.

The more she learned about the island, the more she felt like she learned about herself. She felt she unearthed new pieces of herself every time she learned something new about it. Stepping foot on its ground today was like walking into an old childhood home. The past was alive all around her, calling out to her. She felt like she wanted to know everything about it, all its past, her family's history before it slipped away forever.

"I went to the island today," Eden said, unable to hold it back any longer. Her grandmother's eyes darted up to meet Eden's eyes, they were full of curiosity and pain. She stared at her for a moment, unsure how to respond.

"And what did you see?" she asked, not wanting to know the answer.

Eden took a breath in, "there wasn't much left. We did find a graveyard and a house. It still had some furniture and dishes inside."

"Mhm," her grandmother replied trying to sound interested. Eden couldn't understand why her grandmother seemed to want nothing to do with the island.

"And, I met someone," Eden paused before continuing. "He said his grandfather used to live on the island the same time you lived there." Her grandmother looked out the window, out at the people gathered in the backyard, the party, and smiling faces unaware of the conversation going on inside.

"What was his name? The grandfather's name, did you ask him?" Her grandmother leaned in, her eyes filled with a curiosity that she usually kept suppressed. It was as if she had always locked it away, fearing that it would consume her like a restless beast pulling and gnawing at her from within.

"I didn't, I'm sorry. I'll have to go back and see if Hudson is there. That's the boy I met. He did say that his grandfather came to Holland Island to be a fisherman, he said he came from another island, I can't remember." Eden's voice trailed off as her brain strained to remember.

"Smith?" her grandmother asked, curious and hopeful.

"Yes! That was it!" Eden said, pointing to her.

"Well," her grandmother said, in a low, quiet tone. "There were quite a few people that came to our island from Smith Island, I didn't know them all." She said, shutting down the curiosity that had tried to reach its way out, closing it back up, and putting it back where it belonged.

Eden saw that her eyes fell again; the curious spark had died back down. *Why hadn't she asked the grandfather's name?* she thought. *Stupid, stupid girl.* "I was thinking I'd like to go back, now that summer is here and I'm done with school for now, and I was thinking it would be fun if you came with me?" Eden said excitedly, trying to reignite the spark that was in her grandmother's eyes just a few moments ago.

There was no answer. Eden knew asking her grandmother to go with her was a very big ask, but she figured why not try. Eden was sure that her grandmother knew more about the island than anyone. She believed that if she could only convince her grandmother to return to the island and stand on the ground where she was born and raised, it would reveal many hidden stories and memories, bringing back the forgotten faces and names of the people who used to live there.

Eden's grandmother looked at her granddaughter's face, so full of hope and expectation. She could see how desperately Eden wanted her to do this. But how could she go back to the most wonderful but painful place she had ever known? How could she stand on the ground and open the door to the memories that she spent so many years trying to forget?

"I don't know my dear. I will think about that, I promise," she said with all the reassurance she could muster up, as she patted her hand. "You should go back outside and have fun with your friends, drink a beer for me, and get a good buzz!" she said with a wink and a smile.

Eden dropped her head and let out a small chuckle in defeat, "ok grandma, you got it!" Eden said as she stood up, she leaned down and kissed the top of her grandmother's gray-haired head. "I love you!" Eden said as she went out the back door.

"You too, my girl," her grandmother said, with a smile, small tears welled at the corners of her eyes. She let out a long sigh, feeling the guilt of her answer.

Chapter Thirteen

Hattie 1917

Winter arrived suddenly and without warning. Unseasonably cooler temperatures spread across the country in early November. A cold snap took over areas as far as east of the Rockies affecting the harvest period. Crops did not have the chance to properly grow and many of them had been damaged or spoiled, affecting much of the country. To add to those hardships, a heating fuel crisis was also hitting the country with coal in short supply. Trains, already overburdened with supplies for the war effort, were having a difficult time transporting goods to many parts of the country. At the beginning of December, the Northeast was pelted with rain followed by a 10-day freeze. Towards the middle of the month, snow began to fall and didn't stop for days. Rivers and ponds were frozen solid. Miles of the shallow outlying waters of the bay were frozen, making it very difficult for fishing or harvesting of any kind. Only a handful of families remained on the island. The community center closed, as well as a good number of the shops and supply stores. Homes were packed up and shipped off on barges and some were left abandoned, just a shell of what once was, and a foreshadowing of what was coming.

Hattie helped her mother with busy work, mending holes in clothes, and canning what little they could harvest. Her hands were busy with tasks around the home, but her mind was with Wes. They had been seeing each other whenever they could. Sneaking out in the night, stealing kisses behind the shed, holding hands while they walked along the shoreline. The blustery, harsh winter had killed a lot of things, but their young love had blossomed and grown.

Hattie felt a deep ache for Wes when she wasn't with him. She found it hard to focus on anything else, constantly daydreaming about his touch, his kisses, and his smile. They hadn't given themselves to each other sexually yet, but Hattie couldn't help but fantasize about what it would be like. Her stomach did a somersault just thinking about it.

Was Wes thinking the same thing? she thought. *Did he desire and dream about me the way I do for him?* It had been days since Hattie had seen him and she ached for him. She was hopeful that today she could get out for a while to see if she could find him.

Hattie finished up her chores and told her mother she was going to meet up with a friend on the island.

Her mother was preoccupied and simply said "Ok, be home for supper," without pressing or questioning her. Hattie's mother's response both surprised and delighted her. She quickly put on her sweater, coat, mittens, and hat. She slid on her heavy black rubber boots over her thick wool socks. She would need all the extra warmth she could get. She hurried out the back door and walked along the shore, her eyes scanning for Wes' boat. She walked a good 20 minutes, her boots crunching in the ice and snow beneath her feet, plumes of her breath lingered in the air when she breathed, her nose pink from the cold, but she didn't care. She stopped when she spotted him, he was breaking up the ice around his boat, trying to harvest whatever he could get, his net held just a couple of moonshine and ninigret oysters. He chipped away at the ice using a pick, his muscles showing off through his coat as he raised it above his head and slammed it down against the ice. Hattie ran towards him as fast as she could, trying her best not to slip and fall on the snow and ice. He stopped and turned toward her, his face slowly realizing it was her, gave way to a wide smile, he let out a chuckle and his breath plumed in the air around him. He dropped the pick in the ice and caught her as she jumped up into his arms.

His strong forearms supported her from underneath, their lips met in a passionate kiss. The warmth from their mouths warmed Hattie from head to toe. Butterflies took flight in her stomach as their tongues swirled and danced inside of each other's mouths, warm and sweet. She gave a little moan of pleasure and it surprised and delighted Wes. He pulled back and looked her in her eyes.

"Hello," he said softly.

"Hi," she said with a wry smile. "I missed you so much, I had to come find you and get my hands on you," she said in between soft, little kisses that she planted on his cheeks and neck.

"My, my, how forward you are!" he said with a chuckle. "I like it, you can come find me anytime, it sure beats breaking ice and looking for oysters." She smiled at his response and got down from his arms. He took her face in his hands and kissed her long and slow.

She leaned in and whispered in his ear, "I want you completely."

He pulled back and stared at her, eyes searching hers, "You sure?" he asked, shocked and serious.

"Yes, I'm sure," she said with a warm smile. "I have something for you," she said. She reached into her coat pocket and pulled out the pocket watch, she reached for his hand and placed it in his palm.

He stared at it, turning it over in his hand, his fingers touching and tracing the intricate design of the gulls flying over the ocean. "This is beautiful Hattie, this must have cost a good bit of money, I can't accept this." He said, handing the watch back to her.

"Nonsense! I want you to have it." she said as she closed his fingers over the gift. "I got it when we were in Cambridge. I decided I would give it to you when I was ready to…" her voice trailed off, unable to say the words. She looked him in the eyes and smiled shyly.

He put the watch in his pocket, kissed her on the forehead, and whispered, "Thank you."

He took her hand and grabbed his ice pick and net of oysters and they headed towards the shed at old man Tom's house. Wes peeked through the back window. Tom was sound asleep on the couch. They quickly hurried into the shed, closed the old wooden door behind them, and placed a crate in front of it, just in case Tom wandered out of the warm house. Wes placed the net and pick on the shucking table and made a small fire in the old black stove that sat in the corner. They used it to boil water for canning and to keep them warm during the long cold winter months. Hattie took some burlap sacks and a blanket from the shelves and placed them on the floor. The light from the fire shone and flashed around them, the light dancing across the walls casting a warm glow throughout the small room.

Hattie sat down on the blanket, shaking slightly from the nerves that rattled through her. Wes crossed the room and sat down next to her, he took her face in his hands and kissed her, soft and warm, trying his best to reassure her. Her hands slid up under his shirt, still slightly shaking and cold. Wes let out a small yelp at the touch of her chilly hands on his warm chest.

She smiled and whispered, "Sorry, I need to warm them up."

"It's alright," he said, lips still against hers. "I will warm you up," he said smiling. He took his hands from her face and started exploring her body. His eyes gleamed and danced in the firelight, completely in awe and wonder as she removed her clothes one by one. He sucked in a breath as he took her in, and touched her soft, pale, perfect skin. She quivered under his touch, wanting it, but also tensing from the newness of being touched and exposed for the first time. Slowly he did the same, removing each piece of clothing until they were both bare, completely vulnerable, and exposed to each other. And there, by the light of the fire, on blankets on the floor, in a small old shed, worn and faded by the weather, they gave themselves to each other.

Hattie sat by the crackling fire that evening in the living room with her brother, staring at the flames that rose and fell, they lit up her face and warmed her cheeks. Her mind replayed what happened earlier. Her stomach turned and flipped at the thought of Wes. The way his hands felt on her skin, the way he felt inside of her, the warmth of his body against hers.

"Think we'll stay here until our house falls into the bay?" Ollie asked her in a whisper. His words snapped her out of her daydream.

She thought about the question, and let out a slow sigh, "I don't know." She replied, sad and low. The thought of leaving this island was once her dream, it was the only thing she cared about, all she ever wanted, but now, it made her want to cry. The thought of being anywhere but with Wes was excruciating, her eyes brimmed with tears at the thought.

"All my friends have already left, it's not home anymore," Ollie said, as his voice strained against the cry that threatened to let out. Hattie and Ollie sat by the fire long into the night and stared at the flames as tears spilled down their cheeks.

The next morning Hattie woke to find her father in the kitchen cooking eggs on the stove, something she hadn't seen a day in her life. He stood with his back hunched over the stove, somewhat frail and broken from the hard work of being an oysterman. For the first time she saw the effects of island life displayed on her father's body. She saw her father differently in that moment; he seemed fragile, and human, whereas in the past she had always seen him as a pillar of strength, unshakable against the elements of the bay.

"Morning papa," she said softly. "Where's mama?"

He turned and faced her but continued to stir the eggs.

"She's gone to the mainland. Will you get some bread out of the cupboard, and we'll toast it up." Hattie's eyes grew large at his words and how he could so casually say them. She crossed the kitchen and got the bread from the cupboard.

"What do you mean she's gone to the mainland?" Hattie said, trying to remain calm.

"She's gone to Edgewater to help at the base hospital there. The soldiers there have got the Spanish flu, and they're calling in help from anyone who can lend a hand in helping them get better." He pointed to a letter that lay open on the table. "See for yourself."

Hattie picked up the flyer and looked at the nurse in uniform on the front. This woman in the picture, heroic, a symbol of strength and courage, a symbol that was associated to her mother was so foreign to her. She felt a sense of bewilderment but also pride. She didn't know this version of her mother, but she felt honored to be her daughter.

Nurses Are Needed Now!

FOR SERVICE IN THE
ARMY NURSE CORPS
IF YOU ARE A REGISTERED NURSE AND NOT YET 45 YEARS OF AGE
APPLY TO THE SURGEON GENERAL, UNITED STATES ARMY,
WASHINGTON 25, D. C., OR TO ANY RED CROSS PROCUREMENT OFFICE

She flipped it over and read the note typed out on the back.

"Dear Mrs. Amelia White,
Your skill set has been requested at Aberdeen Proving Ground in Edgewater Maryland. Many of our soldiers have fallen ill and need immediate medical attention. We are in desperate need of nurses immediately as many of our nurses are serving their country abroad. Your country is counting on you.
Sincerely,
Brigadier General Colden Ruggles

Sitting next to the letter was a handwritten note from her mother, that read,

"My dearest Hattie and Oliver,
Don't fret about me. I will be home as soon as I can.
We all must do our part to help those in need.
Be good and help your father. I'll see you soon. I love you both.
-Mama"

Chapter Fourteen

Wesley 1917

The winter lingered and hung around long into the beginning of the spring months, like a heavy, dark, cold blanket, clouding the blue skies and sunshine. But slowly and softly the Chesapeake Bay began to shake off winter. The weather turned warmer, the ice and snow slowly melted, and the bay became alive again, opening its sleepy eyes from winter's slumber, and becoming wide awake to spring. The birds soared above, squawking and playing in the sky, dipping and diving in the frigid water. The turtles and frogs mated and multiplied in the outlying shallow waters. The ducks returned and built their nests, laying their eggs and waiting for new life to arrive. The tall grasses began to emerge from the cold wet ground, popping up in a vibrant green, filling the air with an earthy newness. The warmer weather gave hope and life to the island, which was much needed.

Wes couldn't help but think of Hattie, everywhere, everything reminded him of her. The water glistened and reflected shades of blue, like her eyes. The golden long grasses that swayed with the breeze, like her hair. Every oyster he pulled from the bay reminded him of the oyster girl, his oyster girl. How was it possible that she seemed to wrap herself up in everything, weaving into the folds of his everyday life, casting herself as the lead role in the story of his future. The night in the shed had cemented them to one another, bound them together and now she consumed his every thought and desire. Wes knew without a doubt that he needed Hattie in his life forever. She was the only thing that mattered to him now, even if that meant leaving the island to be with her. She had made it clear that she wanted to leave Holland Island when they first met. And if that was her dream and desire, then he would do everything in his power to support that and make it come true, but he was going to do it with her. He would miss this beautiful place so much but the desire and longing to be with her were greater than his desire to stay here without her.

He was hard at work, shucking oysters in the shed, the very shed that they had given themselves to each other in. He picked up a large oyster from the net and placed the tip of the knife on either side of the hinge. Using a good amount of pressure, he pushed the knife into the hinge, and then he twisted the knife from side to side and pried the shell open. There in the center of the oyster was a glistening, white pearl. He picked it up, and cleaned it off, holding it between his pointer finger and thumb. He held it up to the light and examined it. It would be perfect. It was just the right size, color, and shape, all he needed was some wire. He would make a ring for his Hattie, give it to her, and tell her that he wanted to be with her forever, that they could leave the island and go make a life together in the city.

He hadn't seen her in a while. Hattie had taken on the roles and responsibilities of her mother. Tending to the laundry, dishes, cooking, and cleaning, mending her father's and Ollie's clothes, and trying her best to help him with schoolwork since the schoolhouse had closed. Wesley had seen the toll it was taking on her, the bags under her eyes and her already small frame looked even more slender. He wanted to help, he wanted to be there for her and her family, but old man Tom had fallen sick that winter and needed Wes to tend to him and continue harvesting and fishing and tending to the property. Oyster season was quickly coming to an end, and he had to make the most of these final days in March. He would see her soon, he thought to himself. Just a few more days and he would make it a priority to go be with his girl, to hold her and kiss her, to tell her all the plans he had thought of. He finished up shucking, cleaned up his tools, tossed the empty oyster shells, closed up the shed, and with his perfect pearl tucked in his pocket, headed inside to tend to old man Tom.

The scent of burned stew hit his nostrils the moment he opened the back door. Wesley's stomach dropped, and his breath caught in his chest. Old Tom never let the stew stay on the stove too long. It was the one dish he had allowed his late wife to teach him and prided himself on it. Wes removed the pot from the stove and set it in the sink, then headed into the living room, the fire was only embers now, with a low glow in the center of the pile of black, charred wood. Tom lay motionless on his back on the old worn sofa under a wool blanket, his face was peaceful and still, his gray/white hair peeked out under his wool cap, and there was no rise and fall in his chest. Wes touched his hand and immediately pulled back slowly. Tom's body was cold. Wes let out the breath that he had been holding in and sat down beside the man who had taken him in when he needed it most, the man who taught him that life can still go on after death, the man who had helped him find his way again, the man who encouraged him to open his heart to love and to be loved. Wes placed his hand on his friend and silently said goodbye as he let the tears fall.

Wes' boots squished in the mud as he made his way to Hattie's home. He tapped on the backdoor, and then slid his hand back in his pocket. The wind whipped at his face, blowing his hair around. Ollie opened the door, his eyes bright and cheerful.

"Hey, Wes!"

"Hey Ollie, is your dad around?"

"Yeah, I'll get him, he's sitting in the living room reading the paper, come on in."

Ollie opened the door wide and led the way through the kitchen towards the living room. Hattie was at the stove, cooking minced meat and potatoes for supper. Wes' heart leaped at the sight of her, her eyes sparkled when they met his.

"Wes, what are you doing here? Is everything alright?" Hattie asked, as she set the spoon down and crossed over to him, concern filled her words. Wes placed his hands on her cheeks and gently kissed her forehead. Ollie blushed and giggled at the sight of it.

"I'm fine, it's Old man Tom, he's..." Wesley's eyes left hers and looked at the floor. He didn't want to start crying again. He cleared his throat and continued.

"He passed away this afternoon."

"Oh, Wes, I'm so sorry," Hattie said as she pulled him in and pressed her face against his chest.

"What's going on?" Hattie's father said from the doorway of the living room, his voice stern and low. Hattie pulled back from Wes, feeling slightly embarrassed at the thought that her father had seen them embracing one another. Wes turned to face him, removed his cap and cleared his throat again, his cheeks slightly flushed at the thought that her father had seen them holding each other. "Old man Tom passed away this afternoon. I was hoping you could help me get him to the church for a burial." A silence hung in the air. Hattie's father nodded his head.

"Why don't you sit and join us for dinner, then I'll help you with Mr. Tom," her father said as he pulled out a chair and sat down.

"Thank you, sir, I appreciate it." Wes glanced quickly at Hattie, the two of them making eye contact causing his stomach to flip. Hattie got another place setting and put it on the table in front of Wes. Ollie plopped down in the chair beside him, his legs swinging with excitement. Hattie served each of them a large helping of meat and potatoes and filled their glasses with sweet tea.

"Thank you." Wes said as she served him.

"You're welcome." She smiled and put the pot back on the stove and took her seat next to her father. "Was he sick?" Ollie asked his mouth still slightly full of food.

"Don't talk with your mouth full," Hattie scolded him.

"Yes, he had been fighting a fever and a cough for weeks now." Wes said, as he piled potatoes onto his fork.

"Where did you find him?" Ollie asked.

"Ollie!" Hattie scolded.

"What? Was he just lying on the ground?"

"That's not polite to ask!" Hattie said, glancing at Wes, and then at her father.

"It's ok," Wes said, trying not to laugh. "He was lying on the couch, peaceful, like he had just taken a nap and didn't wake up."

"Oh," Ollie said as he shoveled another bite into his mouth.

They finished up their dinner in silence. Hattie rose to clear their plates.

"Thank you for dinner," Wes said, brushing his fingers over Hattie's as she reached down for his plate.

"You're welcome," Hattie said with a soft smile.

Her father and Wes put their coats, hats and boots on and went out the back door. It was raining lightly now and created more mud along the road.

"We'll have to go to the chapel to fetch the horse and cart first," Hattie's father said. "I'm afraid you'll have to wait to bury him until the ground isn't so wet. We can keep his body in the cellar at the church."

Wes nodded his head.

"So, you intend on marrying her?" Hattie's father said, not looking at Wes. The question took Wes off guard, his cheeks flushed at the question.

"Sir?" Wes asked, his brows furrowed in confusion.

"My Hattie. I am not stupid boy. I see the way the two of you look at each other."

The wind whipped up, howling around them, Wes pulled at the neckline of his coat, feeling uneasy at the sternness of her father's accusation.

"Yes Sir," Wesley said, with all of the confidence he could muster. Her father stopped, narrowed his eyes at Wes, and stared for what felt like hours.

"Good," he finally said, "You have my blessing." He patted Wes on the back and then kept walking. Wes smiled and picked up his pace to keep up with him. *This day had taken quite a turn*, Wes thought.

Chapter Fifteen

Eden 1982

She didn't know if Hudson would be there, but she had to try. She couldn't stop thinking about him since the day she and Melanie met him when they had explored the island for the first time. She couldn't put her finger on why. She had known lots of boys and had had a couple of boyfriends in the past, but none of them ever really stuck. None of them got in her head, sprawled out, and made a home, refusing to leave, none like Hudson. Something about him, something about his calm, deep confidence, his boyish grin, and his innocent charm left her wanting to know more. He had a love and knowledge of the bay that was endearing and somewhat nerdy but also so attractive. She just couldn't figure him out.

Melanie was gone for the weekend. She was off to Outer Banks with her family for the week. Eden went with them lots of times in the past, but this year Eden asked if she could stay back and have permission to take their boat out with a strict rule that she not be out after dark. The bay was an amazing place to explore, but very dangerous at night, even for an experienced and skilled boater.

Eden counted down the minutes until her shift was over at the local ice cream shop in town, the Salted Scoop. She liked her job for the most part, seeing the smiles on people's faces when she handed them their delicious ice cream treat, but there were some not-so-fun moments. The "I wanted a bigger scoop," or the "I said no nuts!" customers were never fun to deal with. But for the most part, it was an easy and flexible job.

As soon as the clock struck 2 pm, Eden untied her bright yellow apron and hung it on the hook. She saw Stephanie walking in the back door.

"Sorry, I got to go! My mom needs me home," Eden told her as she grabbed her purse and headed out the back door. *A little white lie never hurt anyone,* she thought. *It was super slow today anyway, and Stephanie was a stuck-up snob,* so Eden didn't really feel bad about leaving the shop exactly at the time her shift was over. Eden had stayed many times to cover for her, and Stephanie had rarely returned the favor, always saying that she was too busy and had a social life and that Eden should've planned better.

Eden tossed her purse and lunch bag in the basket on the front of her bike and headed down the road toward the dock at Melanie's house. She could feel the freedom and adventure of the open bay as she grew closer to the dock. She loved being on the water, she loved everything about it. The smells, sights, and sounds made her feel alive, she lost all track of time and space out on the water, life was simple, uncluttered, and free. She became a part of it, and she loved that. She leaned her bike up against the brick rancher, grabbed her lunch bag and purse, and ran down the yard and across the dock. She untied the lines, tossed them in the boat, and got in. The engine sputtered and spat as she cranked it. A little smoke billowed out from underneath. She put it in forward and off she went out into the bay, the greenish-blue water lapping against the side of the boat, driving her forward. The salty, seaweed air blew against her face, tugging and playing at the short strands of hair that fell against her face. The gulls flew in encouragement overhead, squawking and calling along the way. A few other boats came into view along the horizon, some fishing, some just enjoying the sun and warm weather.

The mound of green, with its grasses and shallow thin shoreline stuck up out above the water, and the few homes that remained stood in stark contrast against the open bay. The island was losing its fight against the Bay and it broke Eden's heart to see it. The knowledge that nothing could be done, this entire space where people had lived and thrived, made a home, and life was quickly disappearing, vanishing before her eyes. She rounded the corner on the south side of the island, near the house that they had explored last time. Its faded white paint and the soggy green foundation were still standing.

And there, on the front steps, sat Hudson. His faded ball cap was on backward, he wore boots with cargo shorts and a faded Orioles tee shirt, and he was playing the harmonica.

Such an odd soul, Eden thought. *Grown, yet boyish, mature, yet innocent, completely captivating, yet free as a bird.* She could hear his melancholy song quietly in the air as it echoed on the water. When she came into view he stopped, smiled, and raised his hand to her. She smiled and waved back.

The boat slowly tossed about as it grew closer to the shore. She tossed the anchor overboard, removed her jeans, and jumped into the shallow water. Her bare feet met the bottom of the bay, slimy and soggy algae-filled mug squished between her toes, she didn't enjoy that. She walked up the sandy, shallow shore, and closed the gap between them, wiggling and kicking her toes as she walked, sending the mucky sand flying into the air and landing in plops on the ground. He stood, put the harmonica in his pocket, and walked down the rickety, wooden front steps that creaked beneath his weight.

"Hello again," Hudson said with a smile.

"Hello," Eden replied, she could feel her cheeks flush with color, but couldn't tell if it was from the sun or from seeing Hudson again. "Fancy seeing you here again," she continued.

The strands of hair that stuck out from beneath his ball cap blew in the breeze, tickling his forehead. He removed his cap, scratched his head, and put the cap back on facing forward. Eden didn't know why but that motion he just made caused her stomach to flip. *My goodness he was adorable*, she thought as she bit at the bottom of her lip.

"Where's your friend?" he asked.

"She's on vacation with her family in the Outer Banks. They let me use their boat while they're gone," Eden said while trying not to make eye contact with him. She didn't like how quickly she felt herself being so drawn to him. How his eyes, when staring into hers, made her knees feel weak.

"Wanna see something pretty cool?" he asked her, breaking the silence and drawing her eyes to his again.

"Sure," Eden replied and walked over to him.

"You have to be quiet, or you'll scare them," Hudson said as he walked to the left side of the big white house. He crouched down on the ground and motioned for her to do the same. She lowered herself down to his level and looked at him; waiting for him to show her whatever it was that had caught his attention. "See over there," he pointed out at the tall grasses a few yards away from the back of the house.

Eden squinted, looking in the direction his finger was pointing. "I don't see anything," she whispered.

"There, on the ground by the big, bare branches," Hudson said in a low whisper. Eden strained her eyes and looked again in the direction he was referring to.

"Oh, my, I see it!" she said, trying not to be too loud. There, in a mound of grasses and twigs was a blue heron nest. Two young herons with fuzzy brown and gray feathers covered their little bodies; their bright orange beaks peeked out above the nest. They waddled around the nest, stretching and flapping their small wings, making little squawking sounds as they waddled. Eden smiled as she watched them.

"I didn't know herons build their nests on the ground," she said.

"They don't usually. They only build nests on the ground if there are no threats around. The island is a perfect place for a heron to build a nest on the ground because there are no threats of ground predators." Hudson said, keeping his eyes fixed on the nest.

Eden looked at him in wonder and her brow scrunched together in a puzzled expression. "How do you know so much?" She blurted out. Her voice startled the baby herons, causing them to duck low and still in their nest.

"My grandpa," he said. "He knew everything anyone could know about the Bay. It was his passion and he showed and told me everything he knew about it." Eden couldn't help but swoon. The way he lovingly talked about his grandfather was endearing and authentic, honest and vulnerable.

Teenage boys weren't like that, she thought. The ones she had known at school were too cool for nature or family, or anything that had depth. The only thing she found in common or amusing with the boys at school were their love and interest in music. The Eagles, Pink Floyd and Led Zeppelin were the only things she found solidarity and conversation with the hormone filled, awkward and smelly boys at school. Up until Hudson, they were all the same, shallow and somewhat boring. She just figured that's the way teen boys were until they got older and more mature.

She remembered her mother telling her that "girls' brains develop faster than boys, that's why boys seem dumb to you. So, it's not their fault, they're just not at your level yet, give them time." Eden felt like that was a reasonable explanation, but she also found it annoying to have to "dumb down" herself to fit in with boys.

But it was quite the opposite with Hudson. She was the one who felt dumb around him. He knew so much about the bay and the island. How had she known so little about something that she loved so much? But Hudson never laughed at her or made her feel stupid or less than. He simply stated facts and let her absorb them or not, he didn't seem concerned about how she might see him. He was secure in his love and passion for the bay and people either accepted it or they didn't. She accepted it and was feeling herself falling for him because of it.

Just then he looked away from the baby herons and looked straight at her and grinned. That boyish, beautiful smile caused her stomach to do a round off back handspring. *Good lord, I want to kiss that mouth,* she thought. Her thought was so loud she thought maybe he could actually hear it. And as if he could, he leaned forward and met her mouth with his. Her lips encouraged him, softly meeting his and slightly parted in encouragement. It wasn't long or sloppy, it was tender and warm. They pulled back, their eyes holding each other, staring in a surreal, "did that really just happen?" gaze.

"I'm sorry," he whispered.

"Why?" she questioned, she felt slightly week in the knees, but wanted more.

"I don't know, I just really wanted to kiss you, but I didn't know if you felt the same," he explained.

"I do," was all she could quietly answer. His hand rose to her cheek, and he gently tucked a strand of hair behind her ear.

"Then you wouldn't be upset if I did it again?" he asked with a smile.

She grinned and shook her head, "No, I wouldn't mind at all."

Chapter Sixteen

Hattie 1918

The flowers bloomed and the sun began to claim its place in the sky earlier and stay out longer. The summer had arrived in glorious warmth that spread all over, sparkling on the water in the heat of the day. Hattie's mother was coming home any day now. They had received many letters from their mother, telling stories about all about the soldiers that were getting better and stronger, telling them about her daily routine, the food, the other nurses and medical staff that she had made friends with, and about their families waiting for them back home. She had also told them about the hundreds that had passed away without ever getting to say a final goodbye to their loved ones and that terrified Hattie, Ollie, and their father, even though he tried to hide his fear and worry from them. Hattie could see it weighed on him constantly. Hattie's mother wrote about how she felt for every one of them, isolated and afraid, and so very sick. Hattie's mother said that she had made lots of new friends on the mainland and that Hattie would love it there. There were lots of shops and restaurants and activities to do. Her mother described the college in Baltimore, telling her how she saw so many young women like her, walking through campus with books and friends, chatting and smiling, and how she could see her there among them. Hattie's heart sank as she read it, picturing herself there on campus with the other girls, away from Wes. Her mother was describing a way of life that was once all Hattie had ever wanted, but now the idea of it was a dreadful thought that made her stomachache.

Hattie pulled on her light blue cotton dress, tied her hair in a loose braid, and tied it off with a white ribbon. Her hair had grown longer and now hung past her shoulders in soft blonde waves. She felt hopeful she would see her Wesley today and that made her the happiest she had ever felt or known. He had breathed life into her that she never knew was missing, like the thawing of the snow in the warm sunshine. Before him, all she ever dreamed and thought about was leaving the island. Saving every penny and counting down the days until she could find a new life on the mainland. But now, her heart had found adventure, and an unexpected safety, a home in him, and she was completely in love. He was the only thing she cared about now. Life with him was now her vision of the future that she wanted and anything else dimmed in comparison.

After their time in the shack, they had agreed to leave secret notes and small gifts for each other in an old oyster can tucked back on the top shelf in the shack, they wouldn't be seeing each other as much since Wes was busy during Oyster season, doing all the work of harvesting and canning now that Old man Tom had passed. Hattie was overwhelmed and busy herself, fulfilling her role as caretaker in her mother's absence. Hattie checked the can every morning and evening, hoping for something. Over the past few days, she had received a piece of candy, a hairclip, and a note that said, "Thinking about you my Oyster girl." And in return, she had left him things as well, pipe tobacco, beef jerky, and a note that read, "You're all I think about, my Wesley."

But earlier that week when Hattie had checked the can, there was a note that said, "My lips miss yours, I must see you. Have lunch with me on the boat, this Wednesday at 12:30 pm, where we first met. -Your Wes."

Hattie's heart felt like it might burst, it had been weeks since they'd seen, kissed, or felt each other and she longed for him. She finished her chores quickly that morning, peeled the potatoes for supper, gathered what was ready from the garden, and hung the wet clothes on the line to dry in the summer sunshine. *I'll pull those when I get back,* she thought as she hurried to the shoreline where she first set her eyes on Wes.

Ollie was now her father's helper, by his side, every day, helping with the fishing, mending the nets, harvesting, and canning the oysters. Hattie was glad about it, glad that her father wouldn't be alone, but she had to admit that she missed the outdoors, the fresh air, the wildlife, and the daily scenes of the bay. She stopped at the water's edge, her bare feet just barely touching the water. She closed her eyes and breathed in deeply, the sun cascading on her face, warming every inch of her, seeping inside to her bones.

"Are you going to stand there all day?" Her eyes popped open at the sound of his voice. He sat in the boat, just off the shore with his forearms resting on his thighs. His eyes shone blue with the light that reflected off the water. He had a smile that spread across his entire face.

My god, he's stunning, and he's mine, she thought as she smiled back at him.

"Get over here little lady, my lips are lonely," he said as he stretched out his arms and motioned for her to come, the boat rocked at his movements. She quickly waded into the water, to the edge of his boat that sat knee deep. He reached out and pulled her up and into the boat, kissing her face as he did. His hands cupped her face, the two of them taking in each other.

"My god, I've missed you," he whispered between kisses.

"You have no idea," she whispered back. "I thought I was going to die without you, it's been so long." Her hands rested up underneath his arms and landed on his lean shoulders. "How are you?" she asked, as she pulled back and looked into his eyes. There was a small funeral that was held at the cemetery where his wife and daughter were buried. The pastor, Hattie's father, a few fishermen, and Charles Wilson, the general store owner, had attended it. Hattie stayed home to take care of Ollie, he had a slight fever and a cough that day.

"I was sorry to miss the funeral." She said, as she stroked his scruffy cheek.

"It's ok love. You didn't miss much. How's Ollie feeling?" he asked as he clasped his hands behind her lower back, supporting her.

"Much better now, he's back to helping papa with the fish and nets," she replied.

"And you? How's my oyster girl?" he said, soft and low as he pulled her to him, their faces so close that their noses touched at the tips.

"I'm fine, better now that you're here," she answered. "So, what did you bring me for lunch?" she asked, her eyes looking up at him with a playful smile.

"Well! Someone is hungry," he laughed as he sat down and pulled the lunch sack out from under the wooden bench. "Only the finest of feasts for my oyster girl," he said with a grin and a wink. He pulled out a bottle of port wine, a block of cheese, a can of freshly picked crab meat and two buttery rolls.

"My goodness! What a treat!" she exclaimed as she sat down beside him.

The two of them sat and ate in the sunshine, gently rocking back and forth by the low waves of the bay, the boat slowly moved farther away from shore, out into deeper water. They talked and laughed in between sips of wine and bites of food. A heron took flight in the distance, its long, narrow, bluish-gray wings looking angelic as they moved up and down in the summer sun. They both stopped and stared as it sailed through the sky.

"A descendant of the dinosaur they say," Wes said out loud.

"Really? How magnificent," Hattie said softly.

"But then again, so is the chicken." Wes said plainly. They both laughed until their stomachs hurt. They finished what was left of the food and drank the last few sips of wine.

Feeling buzzed and warm from the sun, Wes removed his shirt and shoes. "Join me?" he asked with a grin as he jumped out of the boat and crashed into the cool water. It splashed up all over her, causing her to gasp.

"For heaven's sake, Wesley!" she yelled, her voice ending in a laugh.

"Come on, Oyster girl! Come swim with me," Wes called as he tread water, his arms moving in big circles causing little waves to swirl around him.

"All right," she sighed as she rolled her eyes. "But if we get caught, I'll be in loads of trouble!" she said in a stern tone, her eyes looking around as she unbuttoned her dress, exposing her undergarments.

"Hmm, if we get caught, then I guess I'll have to do the proper thing and marry you," he said, smiling.

She spun around, almost knocking herself over in the boat, her eyes darted to his. "Wesley, don't you joke like that!" She scolded, her eyes searching his.

He smiled, "Alright then, how about I just marry you anyway, even if we don't get caught." He reached into the pocket of his pants and pulled out the ring he had made with the pearl he had found the day Tom died. Hattie stood there in her underwear, her eyes wide, and mouth open.

"You got me a ring?" she asked in disbelief.

"Well, I made it, but yes. I got you a ring" he said, smiling.

"You made me a ring," Hattie repeated with her eyes still large and unblinking, mouth still open.

"Yes, I did," he said, still treading water. She continued to stand there with no response. "You going to just stand there or are you going to say yes?" he asked, half joking.

"YES!" she exclaimed as she leaped from the boat and into the water, her body sending water splashing everywhere. He laughed as he pulled her into his arms and kissed her.

"You sure you want to spend the rest of your life with me?" he asked as he held up the ring.

"Yes, I'm sure! I've never wanted anything more," she said as she took the ring from him and slid it on her finger.

"I'll go wherever you want to go. I promise I'll spend the rest of my life trying to give you the life you deserve Hattie." His words were passionate and serious. Tears welled in her eyes as she held onto him, holding him close, her head nuzzled in his neck.

"I don't care where we go, as long as I'm with you, that's all I need," Hattie said, her voice shaky from trying to hold back the tears that welled in her eyes. "I'll even stay on this dreadful island with you." She said as she pulled back to look at him, a big smile on her face. He threw his head back and burst into laughter, the sound echoing out over the water.

They lay on the bank of the Chesapeake, her head on his chest as the sun set. The large yellow-gold ball slowly dipped into the bay. Their fingers playfully intertwined with each other's. He stroked her arm and kissed her forehead. The crickets sang out in rhythm as the daylight slipped away. The tall grasses swayed in the warm night breeze. *This was heaven*, Hattie thought.

"I wish we could stay here forever," she said, her voice quiet and soft.

"Who says we can't?" Wes said with a smile.

Hattie drew in a long breath.

"The world, I suppose."

"Then it will be us against the world," Wes said softly as he kissed her forehead again. Hattie held her hand up and playfully showed off the pearl ring that now sat proudly on her left ring finger.

"Us against the world," she repeated, smiling with her head nuzzled against his chest.

Chapter Seventeen

Wesley 1918

She said yes. He couldn't stop smiling at the thought. He couldn't help but think about the life that was ahead for the two of them, so strange to think how his life had changed because of Hattie. He never imagined he'd ever get married and have a family. He was a drifter, not belonging to anyone or anywhere, he had come to accept it. He didn't need love or affection because he had never really experienced it, until Hattie. Slowly but surely, she had managed to take down the walls that he had built up around his heart after the loss of his father. Love only opens you up to loss, and he did not like the feeling of loss. But his entire world shifted when he set eyes on Hattie, his oyster girl. The feeling of being loved and loving her in return, far outweighed the feeling of loss, and he would risk it again, his heart exposed and vulnerable, for the opportunity of a life spent with her.

He began planning and prepping, turning Old Tom's house into something she would be proud of. He replaced the tin on the roof where the water had gotten in and rust had begun to eat away at the metal. He made wooden shutters for the house and painted them a robin's egg blue. He repaired the front steps and put new windows on the front. He had plans to make a swing and paint it white so they could sit on the porch and watch the sun rise and set.

They had planned to get married in the fall, just a few months away. It was her favorite season, and they didn't want a long engagement. While other families were packing up and leaving Holland Island, preparing to make a life on the mainland, Wes and Hattie were preparing to stay and make a life here. They had talked about the idea of moving off the island, but it just didn't seem right. Tom's house sat far enough away from the shoreline on the west side of the island, the area least impacted by erosion, so they decided that they would stay as long as the bay permitted. Hattie's father couldn't be happier. He knew he would have strong, capable help with Wes around, and Wes was happy to help. He now found a new family and a sense of belonging in the White family. After the passing of his father and old man Tom, he had felt so alone.

Hattie was the sun and moon of his world now. His tides rose and fell at her pull. She was gentle yet fierce, strong yet fragile, loving yet stubborn. He had never known love like this before. He had loved his father and Tom and had been smitten with a few girls before, but this was different. It was beautiful, powerful, and terrifying. He had lived his entire life not needing her, he accepted life as it was, but now there was this thing, this person he never knew he needed before, and the thought of a life without her would be excruciating and unbearable. He now lived for her, but in the same breath, he would also be willing to die for her if need be. That was this love, not a silly childish love, not an infatuation that would fade soon after the newness wore off. This was a deep, enduring true love. It was something, someone that was worth living and dying for, and that completely terrified and captivated him.

Wes had seen the new stylish Congoleum-painted carpets that were not only beautiful but also practical in Newport News Virginia when he was there last week. He took a trip down south to Newport News twice a year to sell or trade his canned oysters. He would trade for new nets or canning supplies, boat parts or harvesting tools. He had seen the artistic rugs on a poster in the furniture store window and couldn't help but think of how much Hattie would love them in the kitchen of their soon-to-be home. The wood floor in the kitchen at Tom's house was worn and rough, almost completely missing in some spots. *How nice it would be to have one of these pretty new rugs to cov-*

er the floor in the kitchen, he thought. *I'll save up and surprise her as a wedding gift, he decided.*

Over those next few weeks, he made extra trips to the mainland, selling canned duck, crab, and oysters. The profit was good, and people needed food. The Spanish flu combined with the war in Germany had taken a toll on the American people. Many homes were without fathers, mothers, and siblings taken too soon. A ready and easy meal, like canned oysters and crab was a treat and a value to those who now struggled to find food.

The sun was just beginning to rise over the bay when Wes woke that morning. Clouds began to form on the distant horizon, he hadn't seen or heard any chance for storms the next few days but August on the coast was unpredictable and reckless. Swells could form out of nowhere and swallow boats whole, leaving them in wreckage on the bottom of the Bay. He pulled his pocket watch out of his pocket and looked at the time as he contemplated waiting to see if the clouds would grow, but the sun was already forcing its warmth, casting a red-orange backdrop across the sky.

It will be a quick trip, and I'll keep the shoreline in view, he thought, as he loaded his boat, untied it from the dock, tossed the lines in the boat, and jumped in. The frogs and katydids sang out in a rhythmic tempo as he rowed away from shore. The swallows and gulls flew overhead, squawking and dipping near the water as they flew, a dove cooed softly in the distance. *The sounds of the Chesapeake*, he thought. This was his favorite time of day on the Chesapeake. It was still, and quiet, the calm before the busy and bustle of the day. You could hear yourself think, you could make sense of things. The entire world seemed to be still, and take a slow, deep breath out here, and he loved it. It was a part of him; the sky, marsh and water were as much a part of his DNA as his skin and bones. People from around here either loved it or left it. He was so grateful and relieved when he and Hattie had decided to stay on the island. He felt a sense of pride knowing that he had begun to open Hattie's eyes to the beauty and privilege of living here; even if she never admitted it, he knew she had. He had seen the way she stared at the sunsets now, how she gently ran her fingers through the tall pampas grass, how she now pointed out the heron nests and fish that jumped out of the water. He had fallen in love with this part of the world and although he was willing to leave it, he was so glad he wouldn't have to.

He left a note and a new satin yellow ribbon for her hair in their oyster can last night, he knew she would worry and wonder where he was if she happened to come by and not see his boat. The note read,

"I've gone to Newport to sell more goods, I'll be back in a few days, don't worry. I can't wait to live every day with you. All my love, -Your Wes."

Chapter Eighteen

Eden 1982

The sun was just starting to set, casting its brilliant colors across its canvas. Eden and Hudson lay on the sandy shoreline watching the sky. Eden's head was snuggled in the crook of Hudson's shoulder and chest.

"I better get going before it gets too dark," Eden said, her voice soft and lazy.

"Yes, you should. The bay can be scary at night," Hudson replied as he kissed the top of her head. They sat up, Hudson standing up first. Then he bent over and put out his hands to help Eden stand up. *Such a gentleman,* she thought.

"Thank you," she said as she held his hands and stood up. They interlocked their hands as they made their way to the shoreline where their boats sat, half on the rocky ground, and half in the water. Hudson helped her into the boat and leaned in to give her a goodbye kiss.

"When can I see you again?" he asked.

"I don't know. Do you want to come to Ridge sometime?" she answered with a questioning smile.

"Yes, actually I would love to," he said.

"Alright then, you free this Saturday afternoon?" she asked.

"I think so, I'll check with my mom," he answered. She grabbed a pen and ripped off a scrap piece of paper from the boat manual, jotted down her address and phone number, and handed it to him.

"Here, call me and let me know," she said with a smile.

"Thanks," he said as he took the piece of paper, glanced at it, and then tucked it in his pants pocket. "You better get going," he said as he kissed her again, and stepped back and pushed her boat into the water.

"I'll see ya later!" she called out and blew a kiss in the air as she started the engine and sputtered away, little plumes of smoke billowing up behind her.

As she made her way across the bay, the sun quickly descended below the horizon, as if it were challenging her to a race. Her heart picked up speed and began to pound harder in her chest. She wasn't scared of the bay, but she was nervous to be out on the open water after dark. The wind was picking up and clouds began to cluster together across the darkening sky. She couldn't figure out where she was. She had a map and landmarks that helped her navigate her way to the island during the day, but everything looked so much different in the dim, dusk light. Her eyes tried to adjust, as they glanced between the dark land, the sinking sun and her depth finder.

Her eyes searched for familiar landmarks, when suddenly, her boat slammed into something hard, her body lurching forward as the engine shut off. Confused and bewildered she looked around, the depth finder indicating she was on the ground. A sandbar, she had slammed head-on into it and had no way of getting off.

Well, I guess I'll be sleeping on the Bay tonight, she thought, as she looked around for any sign of another boat nearby but saw no one. She removed the seat cushions, looking for a flare, but there were none. She sat and waited for what seemed like hours, her eyes growing tired from straining to see in the dark. No one was out there, no one was coming. She found some life jackets, placed one behind her head and made herself as comfortable as she could. The boat secured and standing still on the sandbar, the water gently lapped against the side of the boat, lulling her to sleep.

The sun was just beginning to rise as her eyes slowly began to open. It took her a few minutes to realize where she was. She sat and immediately felt a strain in her neck from sleeping in the strained position. She looked around and quickly realized she was not where she was when she had fallen asleep. The tide must have risen and carried her off the sandbar.

She was now just a few miles from the shoreline, but what shoreline she had no idea. She quickly started her engine; it sputtered and spat as it turned over. The noise abrasively broke the still, quiet of the early morning. The wildlife around her responded to the noise, seagulls took flight from their posts on the docks, squawking and calling out as they flew.

She made her way to the shore of somewhere; she didn't know, but she knew she needed to find out before she could figure out how to get home. She pulled up to a vacant dock, killed the engine, and tied her lines to one of the pillars. She made her way down the dock and spotted a quaint, navy blue cottage-style house with a sign that said, "Sarah's on Smith Island, Bed and Breakfast." The home was like a smile, welcoming her in. She walked up to the cheerful home and knocked on its bright red door, hopeful that someone was home and hoping that she wasn't disturbing whoever was inside.

A few minutes later a woman appeared behind the glass panel of the door, opened the door and the smell of fresh baked blueberry muffins and coffee filled the air around the woman. She had blonde hair and dimples that appeared in the corners of her round, pink cheeks as she smiled.

"Hello, can I help you?" the woman asked.

"Yes ma'am, I'm sorry to bother you so early, I ran into a sandbar last night when I was trying to get home in the dark, I spent the night on my boat and was wondering if you could tell me where I am, and if you knew the best way to get to Ridge, Maryland? And if you had a bathroom I could use?" Eden asked, her voice slightly shaking.

"Oh, my heavens child! Yes! Come in, come in," she said cheerfully as she stepped aside and ushered her into the foyer. The quaint little bungalow had hardwood floors and floral-papered walls. Lace curtains hung from the windows allowing the sun to shine through, casting patterns on the hallway that lead to the bright sunroom towards the back of the home.

"The bathroom is the first door on the left, help yourself," the woman said as she motioned down the hallway.

"Thank you very much," Eden replied as she walked past the woman and towards the bathroom.

"Come to the sunroom when you're finished, I'll have a warm muffin waiting for you," the woman said with a smile and a wink, as she walked towards the back of the house.

The sunroom was warm and cozy. Wooden rockers and a white wicker sofa aligned the room, with pale blue cushions that looked soft and inviting. The windows that lined the room framed the bay and all its beauty. The sunrise was glowing yellows and oranges, casting its colors on the water. The colors moved and danced as the water rippled and moved. Grasses swayed in the early morning breeze, two Adirondack chairs sat together by the shoreline, welcoming travelers to come and sit and relax.

"Come have a seat honey, you must be hungry," the woman said as she set a plate with a buttered muffin and cup of coffee on the small round table in the center of the room.

"Thank you," Eden replied, grateful for the strangers' hospitality, her stomach rumbling at the thought of food. Eden sat down at the table and began eating the warm muffin. The woman placed cream and sugar down on the table and took a seat across from her.

"Mmm, this is delicious," Eden said with a moan.

"Glad you like it," the woman said with a chuckle. "Welcome to Smith Island." She said, as she folded her hands and placed them in her lap. "Where did you come from?" she asked, her face still holding a smile.

"I was leaving Holland Island at sunset yesterday and was heading home to Ridge, Maryland, I think I was about halfway home when I ran into a sandbar." Eden replied.

"Holland Island, What on earth were you doing there?" the woman asked.

"I was exploring it. My grandmother was born there and grew up on the island. I had heard stories of it and wanted to see it for myself," Eden said as she stirred in sugar and lots of cream into her coffee and took a small sip, the steam rising up and around, tickling her nostrils.

"I see. That's quite brave of you to go across the bay and explore an island all by yourself," the woman replied, shocked in her tone.

"Oh I wasn't alone, I was with a friend, his grandfather lived on the island too," Eden said she took another sip of coffee and then set it down on the table.

"Well good for you two for wanting to see where you come from. You drifted south from Holland Island. You'll want to head north to get back home." The woman replied, took a pause, and then continued, "You know, if you're interested in learning more about the islands and this area, you should check out the museum just up the street. They have pictures and interesting facts about life back in those days." The woman handed Eden a napkin as she finished speaking.

"Oh, I would love to go see that! Thank you!" Eden explained as she took the napkin and wiped her mouth. "Thank you so much for the muffin and coffee, it was delicious," Eden said as she rose and reached her hand in her pocket to pull out her tip money, she had made at the ice cream stand yesterday.

"Oh, no. Not needed," the woman said as she put her hands up in protest.

"Are you sure? I really appreciate your kindness," Eden replied.

"Yes, I'm sure, I'm glad to help someone in need, you use that money for gas to get home, I'm sure you're running low by now," the woman said as she rose from the table and put her hands on Eden's arm.

"You're probably right, thank you, very much." Eden replied, her words filled with gratitude. "Do you mind if I use your telephone to call my mom? I'm sure she's worried sick," Eden asked.

"Of course!" the woman replied as she led her to the kitchen where the white phone hung on the wall. Eden picked up the phone and dialed her home number. Her mother picked up on the first ring. Eden spent the next 15 minutes reassuring her mother that she was ok and that she would be home in a few hours. She told her of the stranger's kindness, reassured her again that she was ok and hung up.

They walked down the hallway and out the front door. Eden turned back to the woman and said thank you again, smiling and waving as she walked away from the beautiful little home.

"Come back, visit anytime!" The woman called out.

"I will!" Eden called out as she turned the corner of the street. The quaint town of Ewell was just beginning to wake up for the day, the fishermen were heading out into the bay, some to go crabbing, their boats full of crab traps, lines, and floats, others had nets and lines. A few cars drove down the street, a couple walked past on the sidewalk, holding hands and chatting, a lawnmower started up in the distance, the smell of fresh-cut grass mixed with the fishy smell of the bay. The small, lively town made her wonder if this is what Holland Island was like back in its heyday, busy with life and population, thriving with families and people, who made a life, a living, and a home on a piece of land surrounded by the Bay, completely happy to be separated from everyone else on the mainland.

The maritime museum was a small little building that sat on the edge of Caleb Jones Road and the shoreline, nestled next to the Bayside Inn. There was a plaque on a wooden stand out in front of the building that told of the history of the island and of how it came to be. It told of the oystermen and fisherman and their fight against the Virginia wardens to govern how much and when you could harvest from the Bay. It told of the men that had lost their lives fighting for the cause. There were pictures of skipjacks and schooners, fishermen wading in the water with nets and rakes. Then she froze, her eyes stopped on a picture of a man beaming with pride as he held up his catch of a full bushel of crabs. The man was the spitting image of Hudson.

Chapter Nineteen

Hattie 1918

The clouds were almost black in color, thick and heavy with rain. The wind whipped up in a fierce fury, rattling the walls, and tearing metal and shingles from the roofs. Trees snapped and took flight into the air, landing with a thud as the heavy trunks hit the ground. Boats slammed against the docks, sinking halfway into the water, some of the boats' lines snapped from the docks setting them free, drifting out into the open bay, tossing and rolling in the angry waves. Pieces of wood and debris sailed through the air slamming into houses and shattering windows. Storefront awnings tore away from their frames, the wind whipping them up and away into the air.

Hattie sat huddled on the sofa, snuggled up under a blanket with Ollie. Their father had closed the storm shutters on the outside of the house, protecting them from flying debris. Hattie cracked the door and peeked to see what was going on outside. She quickly shut it, fearful of the wind that whipped at her face. Wes had set out for Newport News before sunrise this morning. Hattie was hoping that he would head inland to find shelter or decided to turn around and come back home, but she hadn't seen any sign of him or his boat.

Hattie's mother had also not returned home yet. They had received a letter informing them that she had taken ill the day before she was expected to be dismissed from her duties and that they were tending to her there at the army hospital and hoping for her to be on the mend soon, but there hadn't been any update on her condition for days. Hattie's father, who was usually very good at hiding his emotions and fears, was concerned. He had been easily irritated. He had made plans to go see her and beg to bring her home, but they informed him not to come, for fear of the flu spreading to the small island and infecting everyone. Her father paced all day and kept himself busy; he no longer sat in his chair by the fire at night, too afraid to sit with his thoughts. He busied himself out in the oyster shed, out on the water and in the yard, mending, fixing, and tinkering with anything he could. It worried Hattie. She could see the fear and stress taking its toll on her father. She tried to help him and make sure the laundry was always getting done and food was always ready and warm on the table when he came in from a long day of harvesting and fishing, but the lines and worry remained heavy and deep on his face. Her parents weren't overly affectionate or lovey, but she knew they loved each other. She could see it in the way her mother would hand him his coffee in the morning then softly and quickly drag her hand across his shoulder. Or the way her father stared at her when she was hanging clothes on the line in the summer sunshine, the golden rays catching her silvering blonde hair causing it to glisten like glitter. Or how the two of them would sit together on the porch swing on Sunday afternoon after church and sip iced tea and discuss the sermon or the latest gossip on the island, her mother smiling and laughing as her father made jokes about certain people in town, telling him to hush his mouth in between giggles.

Hattie busied herself with dinner while the storm raged in angry gusts outside. She took out her worry and fear on the mashed potatoes, slamming the masher into them. She whisked the brown gravy too fast causing it to splatter all over the back of the stove. Ham steaks sizzled and popped in a skillet on the stove, adding a distracting contrast to the sounds of the storm that was wreaking havoc on the island outside. Ollie came into the kitchen and took a seat at the table, taking a sip of water from his glass, his face full of fear.

"It's going to be alright Ollie," Hattie said, her eyes fixed on the simmering food she was cooking on the stove. "It's all going to be alright," she said again as she tried not to burst into tears, her eyes stinging as she held back the fear.

Bang! Her father burst through the backdoor, soaking wet, his hair windblown but surprisingly his eyes were bright and happy.

"She's coming home! Your mama's coming home!" he said as he raised the letter in the air, water dripping off his clothes and puddling onto the floor. Hattie dropped the whisk in the gravy pot, Ollie jumped up from the table, both of them ran towards their father and they embraced in a big, wet happy hug and for a moment the stress and worry subsided. The rock of their family was coming home, the void that had been impossible to fill would be back, and for the first time in a while, the air in their home held hope. The storm raged on outside as the three of them sat and ate dinner, their father's face free of strain and stress. Even though it was chaos outside, inside their home was a warmth and a peace knowing that their mother was alright. Ollie swung his legs in childlike joy as he ate his dinner, happy at the thought that he would soon have his mother home again.

Hattie was happy to see her father and brother's smiles back on their faces, their worry and stress lighter knowing their rock, the glue that had held this family together was coming home. But she still felt weighed down thinking that Wes was out there. She tried not to think about him being tossed around in the open water, possibly fighting for his life among the wind and waves. She tried to hold onto the hope that he was fine, that he was safe in Newport, and that he would come home in a few days. As soon as the storm let up, she would go search for him, maybe send word to Newport to see if he had made it.

Why hadn't he stayed here? Surely, he saw the clouds growing dark when he left this morning. How could he be so reckless? Hattie's emotions were running all over the place, going from happiness, to fear, to hope, and then quickly changing to anger. She was a wreck, wanting so badly to take a walk, to clear her head. She wanted to go sit on the shoreline and breathe in the air and calm her anxious heart and mind. *This stupid storm*, she thought as she cleaned up the dinner dishes and tidied the kitchen, banging and slamming the dishes and cabinets. Her back was to her father who was standing in the doorway, watching her.

"You doing ok?" he asked in a low, curious tone.

Hattie jumped, dropping the dish towel in her hand.

"Oh, daddy! You scared me. I didn't see you standing there," she said in a yelp.

He chuckled quietly and sat at the table, pulled out the chair next to him, and patted it with his hand, beckoning her to sit. Hattie reached down and picked up the towel and set it on the counter, then walked over and sat down beside her father. She took a deep breath and let out a long sigh. Her father laid his hand on top of hers and looked into her eyes. She couldn't hold it back any longer, she burst into tears, bringing both her hands up and covering her face, her shoulders shaking with heavy sobs.

Her father didn't shush her, or tell her it would be alright, he simply sat with her and let her cry. He knew how much she loved Wesley; he saw it happen before his eyes. That young man had turned his little girl into a lovesick young woman. He saw the way she ran and jumped into his arms and planted tender kisses on each other when they thought no one was watching. He saw it in the way she lit up like a firefly whenever he was around. Just the mention of his name put a twinkle in her eye. It reminded him of himself and Amelia when their love was fresh and new. He was skeptical at first, Hattie had always been his girl, his helper, and no boy had ever been good enough for his Hattie. But he had seen love and kindness in the way Wes treated her, the way he spoke about her, and smiled at her. Hattie's father also appreciated the way Wesley respected the island and revered and appreciated his life as a fisherman. He never spoke as if he considered this way of life to be inferior or inadequate for himself or anyone else. He had proved himself to be a man of character and he was worthy of her. He had shown it over the last few months and Henry couldn't ask for a better young man than Wes to join their family and take care of his daughter. He knew that she must be worried sick about him, and there was nothing he could say or do right now to ease her fear.

The sun rose with a soft glow the next morning, rain dotted the outside of the window, casting little prisms on the floor and ceiling. Hattie sat up and stretched. She glanced out the window and saw that the rain had stopped, the wind was silent. The storm was over. She jumped out of bed and quickly got dressed, not caring enough to bother with her hair, she let it hang in loose waves down her back. She hurried downstairs and found Ollie at the table with a jelly and buttered biscuit, leftovers from yesterday. She ran past him and grabbed her boots.

"Want a bite?" he asked as he held it up, curious as to why she hadn't grabbed it and taken a bite without asking, the way she normally would've.

The question made Hattie pause and smile.

"Sure, thanks," she said as she took it from him and bit into it, handed it back, and slid on her boots. "I'm going out to see what damage there is, if you need me, I'll be at Old Man Tom's place," she said as she opened the back door and hurried out, the screen door slamming loudly after her.

Hattie froze as she took in the aftermath. The scene was unlike anything she had ever witnessed before. Entire houses were gone. Remains of outbuildings lay in piles along the ground, trees that were older than her, shredded into pieces and laid strewn across the roads and lawns. Damaged boats bobbed in the shallow waters, half sunken from the water they had taken in. Her breath caught in her chest, her stomach in a knot, tears welled in her eyes from the utter destruction. Her feet couldn't run any faster as she took off to the west side of the island, passing the wreckage of more homes along the way. The back half of the schoolhouse was completely gone, the church where they gathered every Sunday was barely recognizable, damaged beyond repair. Pews and hymnals were broken and torn and lay scattered along the streets. The remaining families on the island congregated in the streets, surveying the damage and salvaging what little they could. Betty Combs, the choir director and longtime resident of the island, stood in front of the church, her head in her hands, her shoulders shaking from her sobs.

Hattie's fears tightened their grip, growing stronger by the minute as she witnessed more destruction. Her stomach threatened to empty its contents at the terrifying thoughts racing through her mind about Wes's well-being. She needed him to be at Tom's place, she needed him to be alive and ok. Her heart raced as terrifying thoughts filled her mind. She forced herself to take deep breaths, preparing herself for whatever was next. She turned the corner and ran up the dirt road that led to Tom's house. Hattie stopped as she reached the end of the road.

The house that they were going to make their own, the home they would spend nights together as a married couple, have children, raise a family, and spend forever together, was gone. The only remains of the once-standing home were a handful of bricks strewn about the foundation. Overwhelmed by the sight, Hattie dropped to her knees, tilted her face towards the sky, and let out a heart-wrenching cry.

And worse, there was no sign of Wes anywhere. His boat wasn't at the dock. The shed where they had given themselves to each other lay in a heap on the ground.

Where was he? Maybe he had made it to Newport, maybe he would be home in a few days, she thought, refusing to give up hope yet. She screamed his name; her voice echoed over the water, sending frightened birds squawking into the air. She needed him, needed to see his face, to feel his comforting arms wrap around her, tell her everything would be ok, and that they could rebuild and start fresh and build a new home, a home that they could design and construct themselves and make it just right. But more than anything, she needed to tell him that she was late, he was going to be a father.

Chapter Twenty

Eden 1982

The trip back to Ridge Maryland had taken almost three hours and all Eden could think about was the face of the young man she saw on the plaque at Smith Island in front of the maritime museum. It looked exactly like Hudson, with the same eyes, the same smile, and same wavy, wild dark hair across his forehead. She wished she would've gotten his phone number too, instead of only giving him hers. She wanted to call him as soon as she got home and tell him all about her night and the kind stranger who had helped her, but most of all she wanted to tell him about the picture of the man she saw at Smith Island. She wanted to ask if he had visited there, or still had any family members there. He had mentioned that his grandfather came from Smith Island but hadn't said if any family still lived there.

Her mother was standing on the dock when Eden pulled up, one hand on her hip and the other one up over her eyes, providing shade from the sun. The second Eden jumped out of the boat. Her mom grabbed her and wrapped her up in a hug.

"Thank God you're alright! For heaven's sake Eden, you scared the crap out of me," she said in a panic, pulling her away and holding her by her shoulders so she could look into her eyes. "Don't you ever go out in that boat alone again. Ever!" she said sternly as she pulled her back in against her chest and tightened her hug.

"I'm sorry mom, I didn't mean to scare you, but I'm fine!" Eden replied, slightly rolling her eyes. Her mother finally released Eden from her hug. Eden stepped back and reached back inside the boat to grab her bag and shoes.

The two of them walked down the dock to their faded light blue 1962 ford pickup truck. Eden's mom had inherited the truck from her father after he passed away 8 years ago. Eden's grandfather, Charles, loved that truck. He was a quiet man who lived his life the same way. Showing up and being involved when he had to, but otherwise he preferred to spend his time out on the water, fishing in his little red canoe. Eden was only 10 years old when he passed away from lung cancer. Her grandmother blamed it on the cigarettes that he also loved and refused to give up; the truck still held a faint smell of cigarette smoke.

Eden's grandmother moved in with them after Charles died, it was never a question whether she would or not. Eden couldn't remember a time when she had seen her grandparents show affection for one another, but she assumed that they had at one time fallen in love, young and wild in their youth just like anyone else. Eden had never asked her grandmother how they met or how old they were when they got married, but now she found herself curious about it. Had they met on the island?

Eden loaded her bicycle into the back of the truck and jumped in the passenger seat. Looking out the window at the glistening bay, her eyes grew heavy, she suddenly felt exhausted. The lack of sleep from her night on the water suddenly hit her hard now that she had relaxed.

"You tired baby?" her mom asked as she started the truck, the old engine rumbled low.

"Yeah, I didn't sleep well out there," Eden replied, her eyes closed, and leaned her head against the head-rest. "Is grandma home?" Eden asked.

"Yes, she was baking bread when I left. She was up early, worried about you. You gave us both quite a scare," her mom said, not willing to let Eden off the hook just yet.

"I know, I said I was sorry," Eden said, annoyed, her eyes still closed and her head bobbing back and forth as the truck rumbled down the dirt road.

"Oh, and a boy called for you last night. He also seemed shocked when I told him that you weren't home yet," her mom said, raising one eye in suspicion. Eden's head shot up, her eyes wide in curiosity.

"What did he say?" Eden asked as she looked at her mother.

"Nothing, just that he was wondering if he could speak to you and that he seemed worried after I told him you hadn't come home yet." Her mother gave Eden a side eye, "were you two together out there on the water yesterday?" She asked. Silence hung in the hair after her question,

Eden swallowed hard.

"Yes," she said simply, knowing that things would just be worse if she lied about it.

"Hmm," her mother responded, wondering how far she should press. Eden was 18 now, she wasn't a child anymore, but she still wanted to be involved in her life and she voiced her approval or disapproval of her choices. "Is this the first time you've hung out with this boy?" her mother asked, eyes staring forward.

"No," Eden said quietly. "But the first time wasn't planned, he was on the island the day Melanie and I went out there last week, he's really nice, and knows so much about the island, I think his grandfather lived there when grandma lived there. I invited him over this Saturday, you can meet him yourself," Eden said in a flurry of words, barely stopping to breathe.

"Oh, well ok then," her mother answered.

The truck rumbled up the gravel driveway and came to a stop. Eden jumped out of the truck and ran inside; heading to the kitchen, her grandmother was pulling out a fresh load of bread from the oven. Her long white-silvery hair was in a long braid that hung down her back and tied with a faded satin yellow ribbon.

"Well, there's the wayward wanderer!" her grandmother exclaimed as she set the loaf of bread on the counter under the potholder that was in her hand. Eden walked over to her and hugged her.

"I'm sorry if I scared you grandma," Eden said.

"It's ok honey, just glad you're ok," her grandmother answered as she was released from Eden's hug. Eden went to the fridge and pulled out a pitcher of lemonade, grabbed two glasses from the cabinet and sat at the kitchen table.

"I accidentally ended up on Smith Island," she said as she poured the lemonade into the glasses.

"Oh really," her grandmother said, as she sliced the warm steaming bread on the counter and placed butter on two pieces. The butter instantly melted as it spread across the warm slice. Her grandmother crossed the kitchen and sat next to her granddaughter and placed the bread on the center of the table between them.

"It smells delicious in here," Eden's mother said as she entered the kitchen. She got a glass from the cabinet, filled her glass with lemonade, and joined the two of them at the table.

"Did you hear we are having a visitor from across the Bay on Saturday?" Eden's mother said as she picked up a piece of bread and took a bite, her eyebrows raising.

"Oh?" Eden's grandmother said with curiosity. "Is it the young man you told me about?" she asked, looking at Eden.

"Yes Ma'am," Eden said with a smile. "He is looking forward to meeting you. I think you two have a lot in common." Eden said as she took a long sip of her lemonade.

"Is that so," Eden's grandmother replied with a little chuckle. "Well, I look forward to meeting him too." She said as she placed her wrinkled hands in her lap and stared out the window in the direction of the bay.

Eden felt giddy and anxious at the thought that Hudson would be coming over to her house this afternoon. As much as she tried to conceal her excitement, she simply couldn't. She felt clumsy and preoccupied all morning, dropping her hairbrush, slipping in the shower and spilling her milk while pouring her cereal.

"A little nervous?" her mother questioned while she watched Eden chide herself and clean up the spilled milk on the counter.

"No! Well, maybe a little," Eden snapped back, not wanting her mother to see how much effect the thought of Hudson's expected arrival was having on her.

Eden's mother was more of a friend at this stage in Eden's life. It was more about communication and relationship than parenting. Eden was rarely naughty as a child, sure there were the occasional scolding or being grounded from time to time because of grades but for the most part she helped out around the house and did what she was told. After all, her father had disappeared after he and her mother got divorced when she was 8, and never called or reached out. Eden had seen how hard her mother had worked over the years to provide for them, working 2 to 3 jobs at times to make ends meet. Eden thought her mother, Valerie—everyone called her Val—was a beautiful woman for her age and carried herself with confidence. She didn't weigh herself down with shame after the divorce, unlike some of the other women she had seen. Eden had wondered why her mother had never had a serious boyfriend after her father had left.

"I don't have time for that, and besides, I have you and your grandma to keep me company." She had told her when Eden had asked in the past. But one time when Eden and Melanie were out driving around in Melanie's boat, she saw her mother out on the bay, in a little speed boat with a man, she was sitting on his lap, they were laughing and cuddling in the summer sun. Her mother didn't see them, but she wished she had. Wished she would just tell her that she liked the attention and romance from a man, it would make her feel normal. It would make her feel like she wasn't going crazy for the feelings she was feeling for Hudson. She had considered confronting her mom about it. *But why upset her. Is it really that big of a deal?* she thought. *I'll save the secret and use it; in case I need it one day.*

Eden had never brought home a boy before, well not to meet her mother and grandmother. She had friends, who were boys, over to play and listen to music, but she had never cared or liked them enough to introduce them to her mom and grandma.

"What's all the fuss in here?" Eden's grandma said as she walked into the kitchen. She had on a light-yellow chiffon sundress with pearl buttons and a lace collar that fell just below her knees.

"My goodness! Don't you look nice today!" Val said with a smile. Eden turned from the counter and looked at her grandmother and whistled a catcall sound.

"Oh hush," Her grandmother said as she waved a hand, dismissing them both. She crossed the kitchen and took a seat at the table. Val stood and poured her mother a cup of coffee, adding cream and sugar and set it in front of her.

"What's the special occasion?" Val asked.

"Well, we have a visitor who is coming today, and he's excited to see me, so I figured I would look decent," Eden's grandmother said as she brought the coffee to her lips and slowly sipped it. Eden and her mother exchanged glances at each other and gave a slight smile, both finding it absolutely adorable that she dressed up for Hudson coming over. The three of them sat at the kitchen table, chatting and laughing as they finished their breakfast.

Val was the first to stand up.

"Eden, there's a pile of some things in the living room that I need to put in the attic when you have time today or tomorrow, please," her mother said as she set her coffee cup in the sink.

"Alright," Eden said as she wrinkled her nose in disgust. She didn't like going up in the attic, it still gave her the creeps. Her father told her when she was little that there were ghosts that lived up there, probably to keep her from going up there and getting hurt, but still, she didn't like it.

"I'll be out in the yard pulling weeds from the flower beds if y'all need me," Val said as she put on her sneakers and baseball cap and left out the back door, the screen slapped against the wooden frame after her. Eden got up from the table, took her bowl and her grandmother's coffee cup and placed them in the sink.

"I'll take some more coffee if there's any left," her grandmother said to her over her shoulder.

"Yeah, there is some left," Eden replied. She took the coffee cup and poured what was left in the pot and set it in front of her grandmother along with the cream and sugar and took a seat next to her.

"Grandma," Eden said hesitantly. "How did you and Grandpa Charles meet?" Eden's grandmother took a slow sip of her coffee and looked out the window.

"Well, I was 18 years old, my family and I had just left the island after the hurricane took what little was left of our town." Her eyes glanced down at her hand for a moment, and then she continued, "He lived with his parents next door, here in Ridge. My mother had worked with his mother during the war, they had become friends. He helped us move in since my father's back wasn't working like it should. We quickly became friends and decided that we should get married a few weeks after we started dating. We thought, why not? Life is short," she said with a shrug of her shoulders and took another sip of her coffee. Eden looked at her grandmother's face, trying to read in between the words and lines of the story, and the lack of emotion in her voice and eyes. She was leaving something out of her story, she could tell, but she didn't want to pry too much.

Eden stood and set her dishes in the sink.

"I better go put those things up before Hudson gets here," Eden said as she leaned down and kissed the side of her grandmother's face. She walked out of the kitchen and into the living room, the pile of things that her mother asked her to put in the attic was at the bottom of the stairs, a bag of some old blankets and a box of Easter decorations, the decorations had been needing to go up for months no doubt. She picked up the box and put it under her arm and hoisted the bag over her shoulder and made her way up the stairs and pulled down the drop-down attic ladder. Dust and insulation flow in in the air around her, causing Eden to sneeze.

"Goodness gracious!" she yelled as she waved her hand in the air. She carried the bag and box up the ladder, slowly, trying not to lose her balance. She frantically reached in the dark for the light bulb string, grasped it and pulled it quickly. A shiver ran over her body as she glanced around, a lifetime was up there. A baby crib sat in the corner, stacks of books, and boxes of mementos from the past.

A rustling sound came from the far corner; it scared her, and she let out a scream, dropping the box and bag. Something darted out from behind the corner, knocking over a floor length mirror, knocking it over, and then it disappeared through a hole where the floor met the roof. Eden caught her breath and regained her composure.

She noticed something that was sitting behind the mirror, something she hadn't ever noticed before. She squinted her eyes to see what it was, a small wooden chest sat tucked under the wooden rafter. A layer of dust covered the top of it. Eden walked over to it, placed her hands on the lid and slowly opened it. Dust flew up in the air, the particles dancing in the sunbeams that shone through the cracks in the roof.

Inside was a small stack of folded letters that were tied in a satin yellow ribbon, an old oyster can, and inside of the oyster can was a pearl ring. Eden sat on the floor in front of the trunk, her legs folded underneath her, she held the bundle of letters and slowly untied the faded yellow ribbon. The handwritten letters were frail and faded, but Eden could still read them, every letter was written to Hattie, and signed "-Your Wes," Eden's breath caught in her throat, she felt like she was opening a window into her grandmother's past and witnessing a very fragile, beautiful moment in her life.

Hudson arrived that afternoon. Eden waited at Melanie's dock for him. She had gotten permission for him to dock his boat there while he visited with her for the day. Eden sat on the dock and swung her bare feet just over the water as she waited for him, small schools of fish swam just below the surface, curious in her movements above the water. She jumped up and peered out when his boat came into view, waving her arms to direct him to the dock. She could see his smile as he grew closer, his hair played in the breeze under his backwards ball cap. His tanned face and arms made her long to touch and kiss him.

"Can you catch?" he asked her as he got within earshot. She snapped out of her lusty daydream and wrinkled her nose and furrowed her brows in confusion. He held up his boat lines. "Can you catch a line?" He repeated.

"Oh, sure," she answered as she held her hands out, ready. He threw the first line, she caught it and pulled him in, tightening the line and tied it off. He cut the motor and jumped on the dock, "Thanks," he said, "not too bad for a girl." He said with a smile and a wink and wrapped her up in his arms.

"Hey!" She replied with a playful laugh. The two of them exchanged kisses as they made their way up the dock. They interlocked their fingers, as they walked towards Eden's home, and caught up on each other's day.

"Have you ever been back to Smith Island?" Eden asked.

"Just a few times, to visit my great grandfather's grave with my grandfather," Hudson replied plainly.

"I'm pretty sure I saw a picture of your great grandfather at the maritime museum when I was there."

Hudson stopped walking and faced her.

"Are you serious?" he asked, his eyes wide.

"Yes, the plaque told all about how the oystermen fought to harvest without restrictions, and how some of them lost their lives for it. Hudson, he was the spitting image of you," she said, her tone serious.

"Wow, I'd like to see that. I've never been to the museum. I had no idea," Hudson replied, his voice soft and contemplative. The two of them started walking again, moments of reflective silence passed.

"My grandma got all dolled up for you," Eden said with a smile, hoping to lighten the mood.

"Oh, really?" he replied.

"Mhm, she put on her best dress," Eden said.

"Oh wow!" he said with a chuckle.

"Don't go getting ideas now!" Eden said sarcastically.

"Don't worry, I have my dream girl," he said as he kissed her hand, the gravel crunching under their feet as they walked. Eden smiled at his response. "I mean, how hot is she?" Hudson asked, joking.

"Hudson!" Eden yelled and playfully smacked him in the stomach. They both laughed as they rounded the corner to her house.

Her mother was still in the backyard finishing up weeding the garden. Her grandmother sat on the back porch, a pitcher of lemonade and ham and cheese sandwiches on the patio table. She stood and raised her hand to her mouth as they came into the backyard, staring in disbelief at him, like she was staring at a ghost. Her breath caught in her chest; her hands had a small shake to them as she walked towards them.

Hudson and Eden stopped to introduce him to Eden's mother, he shook her hand and smiled, "it's nice to meet you," he said to Eden's mother. Eden turned and saw her grandmother approaching them, trying to read the look of wonder on her face.

"Hudson, this is my grandma," Eden said as she reached her hand out to her.

"Hello Ma'am," Hudson said as he removed his ball cap and extended his hand out.

Her grandmother cleared her throat, extended her hand and shook his hand.

"It's nice to meet you, young man. You can call me Hattie."

Chapter Twenty-One

Hattie 1918

Hattie sat on the wet marshy ground in the backyard on the shoreline at old man Tom's place, the backyard that was going to be hers and Wesley's. She couldn't muster the strength to stand up, her limbs felt too heavy, her breathing was shallow, her mind refused to comprehend the reality of her life now. It had been hours since she arrived at the property and witnessed the scene, the loss of the future she and Wes had planned and envisioned for the two of them, was now gone. Wes had walked her from childhood into womanhood and he had done so with compassion and gentleness, showing her just how beautiful and wonderful love is and can be. He had opened her eyes to a world of beauty around her, lifting an unforeseen veil that exposed life at its fullest. But now he was gone, and so was the world that he had shown her.

The seagulls called in the distance, the water gently lapped at her feet. She closed her eyes and took a deep breath, trying to feel him, trying to hold onto hope, willing him to come back to her. She felt someone's presence approach her from behind and then sit down next to her. A familiar arm reached around her and brought her in for a comforting hug, her mother's smell filled the air and space around her. Her mother's comforting presence, a feeling and comfort that had been absent for months, was now here, Hattie didn't realize how much she had been holding in until now.

She crumbled in her mother's arms, letting all the worry, stress and fear fall, like big broken pieces around them. Her mother held her tight and kissed her forehead as she cried, and shared with her everything that had happened while she was gone.

"Also, I'm late. I think I'm pregnant. I'm so sorry!" Hattie said. Her eyes were red and swollen, tears streaming down her cheeks. She looked down at the ground, unable to look her mother in the face. Pregnancy out of wed lock was a shame and a scandal and Hattie was worried what news like this would do to her family's reputation. Her mother sighed, then lifted Hattie's chin, forcing her eyes to meet hers. The look in her mother's eyes was a mixture of sadness, disappointment but also understanding.

"You are in love, and while this is not ideal, there is no shame in love. We will figure this out," her mother said, with tears in her eyes as well. The two of them rose and headed back to their home.

That night, Amelia and Henry made the choice to pack up and leave the island over the next few days. There was nothing left for their family here now. The school had shut down, the church was destroyed, and all of the shops had closed. The few remaining families in town had also made the decision to leave. Some of them loaded their entire homes on barges. While others packed light, taking only what was absolutely necessary, leaving their homes a shell to eventually be swallowed up by the bay. The hurricane was the final blow for this small, quaint, beloved Holland Island. The place that they had known and loved, and built a life on was no more, existing now as only memories that would live on in a few photos and stories.

Hattie was restless. Her body was tired, but her mind would not let her rest. Her heart refused to let Wesley go just yet, refused to believe that he was gone. She rose early the next morning, before the sunrise. She had written multiple letters inquiring about Wes and was going to get them to the postman, one to Newport, one to the lighthouse keeper, one to Smith Island. The letters had asked if anyone had seen a fisherman and gave details of Wesley's boat and described him, saying that if anyone knew or had seen anything to please reach out to her with a return address. She got dressed and slipped out the backdoor.

She made her way quickly to her father's skipjack; she had seen him drive it many times and was certain she could operate it herself. She pushed offshore and out into the bay, the water was calm and quiet. The Holland Light house wasn't too far from Holland Island. She had seen it many times when she was out fishing with her father. If anyone could help her, it would be the lighthouse keeper. The skipjack glided through the water; the rising sun cast a warm glow on the small ripples that spread out in her wake. She closed her eyes and drew in a long breath. The lighthouse stuck out of the water like a foreign object. The white screw pile lighthouse with its red roof and black shutters looked oddly out of place as it stood surrounded by the bay. Hattie reached out and grabbed the metal footing of the lighthouse and tied the skipjack to it. She climbed the metal ladder that led to the wrap around deck and entryway of the lighthouse. She drew in a deep breath and knocked. The door creaked open, a middle-aged man stood in the doorway, his hair a sandy blonde mess that swirled in random cowlicks on top of his head. His eyes were a warm brown that looked her up and down, slowly examining her from head to toe. "Can I help you?" he asked curiously.

"Hello, my name is Hattie White, I live on Holland Island. I was wondering if you could answer some questions." Hattie spoke calmly, and slowly, trying to sound confident and sure of herself. Ulman Owens was a known womanizer and was on his second marriage already. He always gave her the creeps and just being near him made her skin crawl. Hattie didn't want to be here any longer than she needed to, and she certainly wasn't going to go inside the lighthouse.

"Come in," Ulman said with a smile as he stood to the side of the doorway and motioned for her to come in.

"No thank you, I'm fine right here," Hattie said, folding her hands as she looked him in the eye.

"Alright then, what is it that you need to ask me?" He smiled seductively and leaned against the doorframe, folding his arms over his chest.

"My fiancé is missing. He is a local oysterman. He headed south towards Newport News the morning of the storm. He has a small john boat. I was wondering if you've seen him." Hattie swallowed hard, trying to suppress the emotions that rattled the back of her throat. Ulman looked her over again, his eyes lingering on her breasts.

"No, I haven't. I'm sorry. The only person I've seen here the last few days is you. You sure you don't want to come in? Have a drink?" He motioned towards the inside of the lighthouse again.

"No, thank you. I best be on my way back before my family worries. Will you do me a favor?" Hattie's eyes met his. She tried to remain confident and strong, even though she wanted to run as fast as she could away from him.

"Anything for you sweetie," he said with an eerie smile.

"If you see him, or anyone who might be him, will you give him this letter? His name is Wesley, Wes for short." She handed him a sealed letter with Wesley's name written on the front of it.

"I can do that," Ulman said as he took the letter from her hand.

"Thank you," Hattie said as she spun on her heels and made her way back down the ladder to her father's skipjack. Ulman walked to the edge of the railing and watched her as she went.

"Come back anytime!" he called out as she sailed away from him. She said nothing as she went back to Holland Island.

By the time Hattie had gotten home, her family had planned to leave. They would move to Ridge Maryland, next to one of Amelia's coworkers that she had met during her time at the army hospital. Amelia had nursed her coworker and friend, Kathryn, back to health when she came down with the flu while tending to the sick soldiers. Amelia never left Kathryn's side while she was sick, spoon feeding her broth, applying a cold compress to her forehead and daily changing her linens.

After Kathryn had recovered, she told Amelia that if she ever needed anything, to reach out and let her know, Amelia had saved her life and Kathryn was eternally grateful for it and wanted to return the favor.

Kathryn and her husband didn't hesitate to offer them Kathryn's mother's home that they had inherited from her when she died. It was a quaint little cottage with a beautiful front porch, a colorful flower garden in the front and vegetable garden in the back. It had three bedrooms and a bathroom. It even had an ice box, which was something the family didn't have on the island. It was also close to the water so their father could still provide for their family the way he knew how. Amelia knew that Kathryn had a family, a son Charles who was a few years older than Hattie and still hadn't married, and two twin daughters, who were a year older than Ollie.

Amelia had shared with Kathryn, in confidence that Hattie was with child, but that it was very early. The two mothers played matchmaker and planned to save everyone from shame and scandal. Plotting and planning to encourage Hattie and Charles to hopefully marry quickly after they meet each other and become friends. It would definitely be a change, starting over would be hard for anyone but it would be a good life, they would have friends and a place to make new memories.

"But I can't leave!" Hattie objected to her parents' decision. "What if he's alive? What if he comes back and looks for me and has no way to find me!" Hattie pleaded.

"I'm sorry Hattie, but we have no choice, we can't stay here, we can't make a life here anymore, there's nothing left," her father said in a matter-of-fact tone. The decision to leave broke his heart just as much as it was breaking hers. "You have a few more days, if he isn't back by the end of the week, we have no choice but to leave." Her mother said softly yet sternly.

Over the next few days her parents and Ollie packed their belongings in crates, taking only what was necessary. Hattie spent every day sitting on the shoreline at Tom's place, her eyes desperately scanning the horizon for any sign of him. She constantly checked the mail for any sign of news from him, nothing. On the third and final day she walked to the desolated property like she had every day since the hurricane. Her feet picked up the pace at the sight of something lying along the water's edge. She recognized it as soon as she got closer. It was the bench from Wes's boat. They had carved their initials in it during one of their lunch dates on his boat. Hattie's heart dropped; she knew she had to accept it now.

Wesley was gone.

Chapter Twenty-Two

Wesley 1918

The storm grew angrier by the minute. Wes knew he had made a mistake going out into the open bay in this weather. It quickly grew more and more furious, Wes searched the horizon for signs of land, but he had been blown out by the fierce wind and waves. The rain made it almost impossible to see, the wind whipped at his back causing the rain to sting like needles as it blew against him. His boat was helpless against the storm, tossing him around like a toy, rising and falling in the pull of the waves. Wes had no idea where he was, or how to get out of the wrath of the storm. The sky grew darker, the waves grew taller, Wes' eyes looked up as an enormous wave started to break over him, coming down hard on him, then lifting him and his boat up, turning it over and over. Wes was pushed underwater, his boat tearing into pieces around him. He struggled to reach the surface as waves pounded and pulled him in every direction. Finally, he broke through the surface, gasping for air, looking for anything to cling to, his arms and legs kicking and paddling to stay above the surface. Just then another wave knocked him under the water again pulling him deeper underwater. Again, he fought against the intense pull of the bay, his eyes stinging, his arms growing tired from fighting for the surface, fighting for air, for survival. He kicked his legs, and made his way to the surface again, breaking the barrier between sky and water, and took a deep breath. A large piece of wood tossed on the surface near him. He swam over to it and draped his arms over it, exhausted. His back heaved up and down as he breathed in and out. He rose and fell with the swells, going underwater every now and then, but stayed near the surface thanks to the piece of wood holding him up.

The sun began to raise, the vibrant, beautiful colors flashing across the sky as if the storm had never happened. Wes had drifted all night, in and out of consciousness, his body draped on the board tossing and turning in the dark, angry waters. But thankfully the storm and the water had calmed as the morning grew closer. Wes felt a hard poke stabbing him in his back, then stopping, then poking again. He slowly and painfully opened his eyes and turned his head and looked behind him.

"He's alive!" shouted a young man's voice. Wes opened his mouth to speak but his throat was hoarse and dry. A fishing boat was suddenly by his side, two men pulling him into the boat, his body landed with a thud on the floor of the boat, Wes coughed and gagged as he rolled onto his side, his skin was purple and pruning from soaking in the water all night long, the water from his clothes pooled around him on the floor.

"Take him below and get him some clothes and a place to rest," a scruffy old voice called out above the others. Two men hoisted Wes up to his feet, draping his arms over their shoulders. Wes' body shook from the air that blew against his soaking wet body. The two men carried and dragged him to the captain's quarters below deck. It was a small dark room with a single bed, a small desk and chair and wooden chest that held a few shirts, pants, socks, and undergarments. They laid Wes on the bed, one of them picked out a shirt and pair of pants from the chest. They took off his wet clothes and dressed him in dry clothes, Wes tried as much as he could to help them, but his arms and legs and lungs were so weak and tired. They finished getting him dressed, laid him down and covered him with blankets, and left the room, shutting the door with a thud on their way out. Wes closed his heavy, tired eyes, and gave into sleep.

Two days later Wes awoke to voices and loud, heavy footsteps above him. His eyes burned as he opened them, he sat straight up, and looked around the small room, trying to figure out where he was, and what had happened. He removed the covers, and stood, taking a moment to steady himself. His legs were still a bit shaky. He saw his clothes draped over the chair by the desk. He grabbed them and changed into them, and then put the clothes he had on back in the wooden chest. He opened the door and made his way upstairs to the deck.

The sun hit him like a warm shower, pouring over his face and skin. The smell of fish, seaweed, and bay water blew in the warm air around him. The gulls swarmed and squawked in the air above as the men on the boat unloaded its large harvest of blue shell crabs. Wes looked around at the shore and the small town that sat along the edge of it. He didn't recognize it, or any of the people that moved and worked around him.

"Well, hello there!" a scruffy, older voice said behind him. Wes turned and saw an older man in worn overalls and plaid shirt with his sleeves rolled to his elbows. He wore a red wool cap and had a gray beard that hung to his chest. His face was kind and cheerful. He had rosy cheeks that stuck out like two ripe cherries above the gray scruffy stubble. He walked up to Wes and patted him on the back, "Glad to see you're alive and well! You must be starving! Come with me, let's get something to eat!" the man said as he walked off the boat and down the dock towards the small town. Wes opened his mouth to speak but the man was already far ahead of him. He quickly picked up his pace and followed the old man.

The old man walked into town and into the Hotel Russell, a large white building that sat in the middle of the town, Wes following quickly behind him. The man walked past the welcome area and into the dining space and made his way to the corner of the room, a bright space with a few tables and chairs scattered around.

"Good to see ya Rusty," A middle aged, curvy woman called from behind the counter. Her dark hair was pulled up in a bun, tied up by a bright red bandana. She had on a white buttoned blouse that revealed her cleavage. Wes stood in the center of the room, taking in the space, the woman and delicious smells of pastries, bacon, and coffee. His stomach rumbled and ached at the thought of food.

"Well, come have a seat boy!" the old man called out as he motioned to the chair beside him. "Two coffees and two breakfast platters please Loretta!" he called out as he leaned back and scratched his potbelly that protruded under his overalls.

Wes walked over and sat beside the old man and smiled hesitantly, as he extended his hand towards the old man.

"My name is Wesley."
The old man reached out and shook Wes' hand.

"Pleased to meet you son, I'm Captain Rusty," the old man said as he let go of his hand. "So, how'd you end up out in the middle of the Chesapeake by yourself?" he asked as he stroked his long, gray beard.

Wes cleared his throat.

"I was heading to Newport News to pick up flooring when the storm rolled in. I was near the coast of Ridge Maryland last I remembered." Loretta arrived at the table with two hot cups of coffee, the steam rose in swirls above the ceramic mugs as she set them down in front of them.

"Who's your friend? A new hired hand?" Loretta asked.

"Nope, I picked this fella out of the ocean, like a drowned cat hanging on for dear life." Rusty said as he picked up one of the mugs and took a sip.

"Oh heavens! Well, looks like you brought him back to life Rusty, looks fine as a fiddle now!" She looked at Wes, who smiled uncomfortably. She grabbed some packets of sugar out of her apron and set them down on the table, patted Wes on the shoulder and then walked back to the kitchen. Wes picked up two packets of sugar, ripped them open and emptied them into his coffee, stirred it quickly and then took a sip.

"Easy now, don't go too fast, you'll make yourself sick." Rusty said to Wes as he took another sip of coffee.

Wes set his cup down and looked at Rusty.

"Thank you, Sir, thank you for finding me out there and for taking me in. You saved my life," Wes said, his words full of gratitude and appreciation.

"Ah, it was no trouble," Rusty said as he waved his hand in the air dismissively.

"If you don't mind me asking, where are we?" Wes said in a low whisper, slightly embarrassed.

"Chincoteague Island, Virginia," Rusty replied, watching Wes' face change to shock. "You were floating on the piece of wood about to be swept out into the ocean, good thing I found you when I did." Rusty said as he picked up his cup and took another sip. Wes sat still and quiet, taking in the reality of what had happened.

Loretta walked up with their warm plates of food.

"Here ya go hero," she said to Rusty as she set it down in front of him. "And yours, survivor boy," she said to Wes as she set it down in front of him. "Anything else I can get you?" she asked as she placed her hands on her round hips. Wes wasted no time diving into his food, and shoveling it into his mouth before she finished her question.

"I think we're good, thanks," Rusty replied with a chuckle.

Loretta laughed.

"Slow down boy or you'll puke it all back up!" she said, her hips swayed, and her shoes clipped on the tile as she walked away. "It's on the house, for saving a life!" She called out behind her as she threw her hand up in the air, the kitchen door swaying back and forth behind her.

"Aw Loretta, you're a peach!" Rusty hollered back. The two of them finished up their food and stood. Rusty reached into his pocket and placed a few dollar bills on the table. "See ya later! Thanks again!" Rusty said towards the kitchen as they walked out the front door and headed back to the docks. "What do you do to make a living son?" Rusty asked Wes.

"Oysterman and a fisherman," Wes replied.

"I'll be heading back inland towards your neck of the woods in the next week or two. You can stay with me and work on my boat to earn your keep for the next few days," Rusty said, his face remaining forward, it was more of a statement than a question.

"Yes, Sir, Thank you," Wes replied. The two of them walked up the dock and joined the other men on board to finish unloading the haul of crabs. Wes' mind drifted to Hattie, wondering if she was ok, if her family was ok, if the island was ok. He wondered if she was worried and looking for him, and if she would be there when or if he made it back to Holland Island.

Chapter Twenty-Three

Hattie 1918

All their belongings were packed into the back of the canvas covered livestock lorry truck. Hattie, her mother, and father sat in the front on the bench seat while Ollie sat in the back of the truck with their belongings. Hattie's father was able to arrange the rental of the truck from a friend who had moved to the mainland a few months prior. It only took a few days to gather the items that made up their life.

How sad, Hattie thought. *How sad that you could pack up your entire life and leave a place, driving away from it like it never existed at all. Was this it? Would they ever return? Would we ever speak of the lifetime that we had here, all the moments and memories, the only life that Hattie and Ollie had known? Or would the moments soon be forgotten and lost, swallowed up and gone like the future of the island?* Quiet tears streamed down Hattie's cheeks as she looked in the rearview mirror. The thought of leaving, the very thought that once was all she wanted, all she strived for was now happening, but she never imagined it would feel like this. In her visions of her departure from the island, she never dreamed that her heart would be shattering, overcome with grief and loss.

"I will never stop looking for you Wes," Hattie said softly to herself as she stared out at the bay and said a silent goodbye to the island.

She had come to love this island, it was where she met the love of her life, where she had first felt and understood the feelings of real love. Scenes of their moments together played like a highlight reel in her mind. Their first meeting, his smile, first touch, his arms, first date, his eyes, first kiss, his lips, first feeling of love, his exposed body against hers. Hattie closed her eyes and tried to hold onto them, trying to commit them to her memory, every single one of them, moments that made her time with Wesley the best moments of her life. No one spoke as her father started the truck and drove away, the gravel road kicked up behind them, leaving their home in a cloud of dust. Hattie looked at her father and could swear she saw tears pooling at the corner of his eyes.

The house in Ridge Maryland was charming and cheerful, it was a buttery yellow with a robin's egg blue colored door and a large front porch. Dahlias, garden roses, and hollyhocks stood in a wide array of colors, bright and tall in front of the porch and lined the walkway. Kathryn and her family stood in the front yard and greeted them with a basket of fresh produce and baked bread when they arrived. The twin girls were giddy and smiling at the sight of Ollie, who jumped out from the back of the truck and offered a slight wave to them, sending the two of them into whispering, giggle fits. Kathryn's husband Robert offered a helping hand as Ollie and Henry untied the canvas stop on the truck. Amelia embraced Kathryn in a warm hug, the two of them smiling and catching up as they walked onto the porch and into the home.

Hattie knew right away what the mothers were plotting, and she had to admit to herself that she would soon run out of time, her pregnancy would become too obvious. She reluctantly made eye contact with Charles. He was shorter than Wes, but he was sturdy, his brown hair matched his brown eyes, he wasn't ugly, but he wasn't handsome, he was ordinary. She couldn't help but be angry, her eyes looking away from him. As much as she knew it wasn't his fault and that she needed to give him a chance, everything in her screamed no. She wasn't ready, her heart wasn't ready, but ready or not she knew she needed to try.

Charles took a step towards her and extended his hand.

"Hello, I'm Charles." He smiled a kind smile.

Hattie extended her hand and shook his, his hands had callouses, and had the wear of a hard day's work.

"Hattie," she said plainly, still looking away.

"Pleased to meet you Hattie," he said as he released her hand, shoving his hands in his pocket, and rocked back and forth on his heels nervously. "I best get to helping your Pa unpacking the truck," he said with a shy smile.

"Ok, thank you," Hattie said softly. A moment of awkward silence hung between them, Hattie's eyes scanned the ground back and forth, hoping he would walk away.

"I'll see you later?" he asked. Hattie nodded, unable to say yes, fearing she would burst into tears at the thought of talking to another man. Charles started walking towards the truck, Hattie's eyes finally looking up at him as he walked away. He stopped and turned back, their eyes catching each other's as he gave her a comforting smile.

Hattie walked up the front porch steps and walked into the place they would now call home.

"Your room is the second door on the right, upstairs," her mother called from the kitchen, giving her an encouraging smile. Hattie nodded and carried her small cedar chest with her clothes up the stairs and to her room. The sun poured into the small but adequate room. In the corner sat a bed that was made with a beautiful handmade quilt, flowers and birds were delicately stitched across the top. Lace curtains hung on rods on the two windows, a small bedside table sat next to the bed, a bouquet of wildflowers in a mason jar sat happily on top of it. Hattie set her chest down at the foot of the bed and walked over to the flowers. She bent down, closed her eyes and took in a deep breath through her nose. Wildflowers like these hadn't grown on the island. Hattie had never seen or smelled anything like them.

"Charles picked them for you," Hattie's mother said softly, she crossed the room and placed an arm around Hattie. "We will all do our best to move on, it doesn't mean we forget the past, but we must try to make the best of the life we have left," her mother said as she gave Hattie a squeeze and a kiss on her forehead. "I know it's hard but give him a chance."

Both families gathered for dinner that evening, the first meal in their new home, a delicious meal of roasted chicken and potatoes, sweet tea, and collard greens. The families chatted through dinner, getting acquainted with each other. The mothers shared stories of their time at the army hospital. Ollie told stories about his friends and life on the island, the twin girls listening to his every word and took turns asking questions. Charles made attempts to get Hattie's attention, occasionally looking at her, smiling after something Ollie said, looking for common ground in her face. Hattie obliged here and there, giving him small smiles and eye contact, her mind and heart at war with each other. After dinner the women cleared the table while the men sat on the front porch and smoked their pipes. Ollie and the girls, Jenny and

Julia, ran around the backyard, catching fireflies in the dusk daylight.

"Go on outside and get some fresh air. Kathryn and I can finish up," Amelia said to Hattie as she took the dish Hattie was drying from her hands. Hattie gave her an appreciative smile and walked out the backdoor to the yard.

The space was wide and lush. *So much green,* Hattie thought. The crickets and katydids chirped in a rhythmic cadence, while the bullfrogs croaked in random bursts. Hattie sat on the back step, closed her eyes and took a deep breath. The warm august breeze blew the wisps of hair around her face.

"Would you like to join me for an evening walk?" Charles asked standing at her side. Hattie jumped slightly, startled by his voice. "I'm sorry, I didn't mean to scare you," he chuckled. It reminded Hattie of the time she first met Wes, Hattie looked down and shook her head, shaking the memory and not letting it linger, trying her best to move on.

"It's alright," Hattie said, as she started to rise to her feet, Charles reached out a hand to help her up. Hattie reached out and took ahold of his hand. "Thank you," she said as he pulled her up. The two of them walked down the gravel road that passed in front of the two homes, and through trees that eventually led to the bay. Hattie heard seagulls in the distance, she leaned her head towards them, her ear straining to hear them. She pulled her head back, slightly embarrassed, realizing how she already missed the gulls' squawking calls.

"Seagulls," Charles said.

"Yes, I know," Hattie said, trying not to roll her eyes at his answer, there was a pause between them after her clipped reply.

"That's right, I'm sure you've seen plenty of them out there on the island, it's just that most girls I've met don't know very much about nature and animals out here," Charles said, slightly embarrassed.

"Well, there's not much else to do on the island but get to know the wildlife and the way they live," she said, forcing her tone to sound kind and understanding. Charles smiled and reached for her hand, grabbing it quickly and intentionally, his eyes met hers. They both came to a stop in the road, Hattie's eyes grew large, her brow furrowed, questioning what on earth he was doing.

"I overheard your mother telling my mother about your... your situation." Hattie's eyes narrowed as she tried to pull her hand free from his. "Listen to me," he said, grabbing her other hand and facing her, his eyes, soft and pleading. "I will take care of you, I promise if you give me a chance, I'll marry you and no one will know, I won't tell a soul. We can raise the child like our own." Hattie's hard expression fell. He dropped her hands, letting his words sink in. She knew this was the best option, not only for her family's sake but for her unborn child's as well. Her heart screamed in protest, pleading with her not to agree to his request, but she knew what she had to do. *She couldn't raise a child out of wedlock; she couldn't do that to her family. If only she had more time, more time to look for Wes, maybe she could go back to Holland Island, maybe this time she would see him, standing on the shore, waiting for her? No, stop it.* She shook her head as her mind fought back and forth. She was so tired of this. *Shut up, he's gone. You must accept it,* she told herself as she swallowed hard. Hattie's eyes fell to the ground. She drew in a breath and let it out slowly.

"I will," Hattie said, her words certain and emotionless.

"Really?" Charles asked, his mouth rose in a small smile as he bent his head under hers, trying to make eye contact with her.

"Yes but give me some time to get to know you, I don't want to marry a stranger," Hattie said, forcing a smile on her face.

"Okay, I can do that," Charles said, wrapping her in an awkward hug.

Chapter Twenty-Four

Wesley 1918

Dozens of horses trotted down Main Street in Chincoteague Virginia. Wes stood on the dock at the shipyard as he watched in bewilderment as the majestic creatures made their way down the streets, past the shops and restaurants, their hooves clicking and clacking on the cobblestone. Captain Rusty had told Wes about the annual Pony Penning, and how they bring the horses from Assateague Island, just north of here, and sell them at auction. The horses lived and bred in two herds on Assateague Island. It was believed that they came to the island after ships wrecked in their voyage to the Americas. It was the island's biggest event of the year; people would come from the surrounding islands. Every hotel room and boarding house was filled, eating and drinking and various festivities led up to the event. Work came to a halt during this time, as the men and women took part in the celebration.

It had been two and half weeks since he first came to Chincoteague on the captain's vessel and Wesley was growing impatient and frustrated. Wesley had held up his end of their deal, he had worked long hours on the captain's skipjack. He had helped the crew haul in nets full of herring, crab and oysters, the work was dirty and exhausting.

"Next week," the captain had told him, but that was last week. Wes was beginning to wonder if he'd ever make it back.

I'll walk if I have to, he thought. Captain Rusty had told Wes that they would make their way back to Holland Island the week following the Pony Penning and this time Wes made him swear to it. Wes feared that Hattie would believe he was dead by now. He asked the captain for an envelope and paper so he could write a letter to send back home. Sending mail to or from the islands was slow and uncertain; he could only hope that she had received it by now, giving her and her family some peace of mind.

"My dearest Hattie,
I am alive and well. My boat was wrecked in the storm. I was picked up by a fishing boat and brought to Chincoteague Island Virginia. I will make my way back to you as soon as I am able. I pray that you and your family are safe and well. I cannot wait to see

your face, to hold you in my arms and kiss your face.
I will see you soon, my oyster girl.
All my love, Your Wes."

Wes had to admit that the parade of wild horses making their way down the main street of Chincoteague was quite amazing and captivating. Men on horseback herded the horses from behind, while onlookers gathered and cheered as the wild beasts passed them by. He saw Captain Rusty standing in front of Hotel Russell, rubbing his belly, full from a recent hot meal no doubt, probably his second one of the day. Wes' stomach rumbled at the thought of food. The captain had arranged for Wesley's meals to be provided for while he was in town, in return Wesley would bring 7lbs of the freshest catch of the day to Loretta.

Wes walked down the dock towards the town, 7lbs of fresh herring, scaled and wrapped under his arm. He tipped his hat to Captain and walked through the front of the hotel, past the welcome desk and into the dining room. He set the fish on the counter and tapped the small silver bell with his finger. The dining room was vacant at the moment, with all of the guests standing out in the street watching the horses. Loretta appeared from the kitchen, hair pulled back in a blue bandana, the hair at her neck clinging to her skin with sweat.

"Well, hello there," she said, wiping the sweat from her brow.

"Hello, busy day?" Wes replied as he pushed the fish towards her.

"Oh honey, the busiest! I hate and love this horse tradition," she said as she let out an exasperated breath.

Wes smiled, "I bet."

She took the fish and headed back towards the kitchen. "Sit anywhere ya like!" She hollered as she disappeared behind the swinging door. Wes sat by the window, he enjoyed people watching, and the event in town made for lots of it. He watched as mothers clung to their young children, smiling and waving at the horses. Fathers hoisted even smaller children up on their shoulders to get a better view. Wes smiled, thinking someday he and Hattie would hopefully start a family, how they would see each other in their children, their love multiplied.

"What can I get ya?" Loretta said, snapping him out of his daydream.

"I'll take whatever is good," Wes said.

"Well honey, it's all good, because I made it," she said with a smile and a wink. Her response made Wes grin, his big, beautiful grin.

"Ok, in that case I'll take the chicken salad sandwich and a sweet tea."

"You betcha," she replied, as she walked back to the kitchen, her curvy frame swaying. She reappeared moments later with his sandwich, roasted potatoes and a glass of sweet tea and set it in front of him. "Here ya go!" she said in a sing-song tone.

"Thank you, Loretta," Wes replied, smiling as he picked up the tea and took a long sip.

"My goodness boy, I bet you have all of the girls swooning over you back home." Wes chuckled at her remarks.

"No ma'am," he said, his dimple on the side of his cheek showing now.

"What?! Of course you do, I wouldn't doubt it for a second," she said as she waved at the air, dismissing his words.

"No ma'am, not all the girls, just one," Wes said in a matter-of-fact tone as he picked up the sandwich and took a large bite, the corners of his mouth still slightly raised in a smile.

"Well heavens, tell me all about her," Loretta said as she pulled out the chair sat down across from him.

"Have some," he said as he slid his plate towards her. She reached out and took one of his roasted potatoes and popped it into her mouth.

"What's she like?" Loretta asked as she chewed and swallowed the potato.

The two of them sat in the hotel window for almost an hour, talking and eating and sharing stories of home and the people they loved.

Loretta had shared how she grew up in Dover Delaware, met the love of her life, Danny, a fisherman who had grown up in the same town as her.

"Danny had a wild side, always looking for adventure but most of the time he only found trouble," she explained. They had gotten married and moved to Chincoteague Island, mostly because the fishing business was better here and the oyster population was plentiful but also partly to get out of Dover, far enough to allow Danny to start over with a fresh reputation. "Danny had a weakness for poker, some people back home had accused him of hiding an ace in his wool cap," Loretta said in a whisper as she leaned in towards Wes.

"Did he?" Wes asked, his brow rose in curiosity.

"Don't know," Loretta said with a shrug of her shoulders. "I guess I never really wanted to know the truth. He promised that if we moved to Chincoteague, he would quit playing poker, said he'd make more money harvesting oysters."

"What happened to him?" Wes asked.

"Well, we moved here in 1901, he made good on his promise for the first few years, but his bad habits got a hold of him again. He started coming home later and later from work. Come to find out he was at the pub gambling again." Wes shook his head and shot her a sympathetic look. "Got into some trouble I reckon. I found him beaten to death in the alley behind our house, an ace of spades lying on the top of his chest," Loretta said as she picked up his sweet tea and took a sip.

"Goodness gracious," Wes replied, shaking his head in disbelief. A moment of silence passed between them.

"After he died, no one cared to look into the murder, said he brought it upon himself, no matter how hard I begged. I did my own investigating and after months of dead ends, I let it go. I was offered the kitchen manager position here at the hotel shortly after, been here ever since." She blew out a long breath and tapped her finger on the table, then fidgeted in her seat, pulling at the cotton dress that clung too tightly to her chest. "I know he wasn't the most admirable man, but my goodness did he have a big heart and a sense of humor. He always made me feel like the most beautiful woman in the world," she said with a smile. Just then groups of people filed in, the ponies had all made their way to the auction corrals, leaving the tourists hungry. Wes and Loretta looked around at the anxious people waiting to be helped.

"Well, I best get these people what they want," she said as she rose from the table.

"I'm sorry about Danny. That must've been awful," Wes said in a low soft tone.

She smiled at him, her eyes glistening with the mention of Danny's name.

"Thank you, honey. I'll see to it that Cap gets you back to your girl," she said as she patted him on the shoulder.

"Thanks Loretta," he said with a smile as he watched her tend to the customers that now filled the room.

Chapter Twenty-Five

Hattie 1918

The early autumn sun cast a morning glow on the backyard. Little drops of morning dew covered the blades of grass that shimmered like diamonds in the sunlight. The soft songs of the black-capped chickadee and the robin could be heard in the distance, their songs encouraging all of nature to wake up. The date was October 1st, a day that was usually marked as the first day of oyster season, was now a day that would be known as Charles and Hattie's wedding day.

Summer had ended and fall was sweeping in, the oranges, yellows and reds had shaded the once green leaves in a glorious autumn display. Hattie and Charles announced their engagement just a few days after Charles proposed the idea on the road that summer night in August. Their families were supportive and congratulated the couple, celebrating the engagement with home churned ice cream and birch beer. Amelia and Kathryn had embraced each other at the news, smiling at their accomplishment of Charles and Hattie's engagement. Hattie's father had smiled at the news, but his eyes held something else when Hattie had stared into them. She darted her eyes from her father's, too afraid to explore what he was trying to hide.

The house buzzed with excitement and antici-pation, cookies and cucumber sandwiches lined the countertops in the kitchen, and elderflower punch chilled in the ice box. Flower arrange-ments of autumn wildflowers were placed on blue and yellow toile tablecloth covered tables in the backyard. Amelia and Kathryn were getting ready to take some of the flower arrangements to the small chapel in town. A few family members from both sides of the families had traveled from various parts of the country by train and were staying at the local hotel in town. They would have their ceremony at the chapel at 11am and then arrive back at the house for refreshments and cake. Charles' father had arranged for the couple to travel from the chapel to the house by a white horse drawn carriage.

"My only son is getting married," justifying himself as he paid the expensive bill for such an extravagant carriage. Ollie and the girls had tied pale blue ribbons attached with empty tin cans to the back of the carriage.

Hattie stood in front of the floor length mirror as she put on her mother's white Victorian lace gown and veil. Her hair was pulled back in a bun that twisted on the sides, small curls at the nape of her neck on the frame of her face. The style was just out of date, but Hattie didn't mind. This entire decision was out of practicality for her. She had chosen to put the memories and feelings of her past deep down inside herself, locking them away.

I will do what is right, she told herself repeatedly as the plans for her wedding and future were discussed. She saved her tears for her pillow at night, for the late midnight hours when everyone was asleep. She swallowed hard, as she stared at herself, the young woman that stared back at her was unrecognizable. The free spirit of her youth had been killed by grief, the wonder and adventure had fled from her eyes, replaced with obedience and resolve.

She played with the pearl ring that was still on her finger, the one Wes had given her just a few months ago. She slowly slid it off her finger and placed it in her wooden chest, her heart welding shut as she closed the lid.

There was a knock on her door, she cleared her throat.

"Come in," she said, her eyes darted to the door. The door creaked open slowly, her father stood in the doorway, his eyes taking in the sight of her in her mother's dress, his baby girl, a grown woman about to make one of the biggest decisions in her life.

His eyes glistened as they welled with tears, "You look beautiful," he said as he entered the room. Hattie turned and faced him, holding back her tears, too afraid that if she started to cry, she wouldn't be able to stop. He put his hands up and cupped her face with his calloused, large hands; her face was delicate and small in his hands.

"I'm going to tell you the same thing I told Charles when he asked for your hand," Hattie's eyebrows raised in suspicion. "Be patient. Give it time, there's no rush," he said, his voice full of love. Their eyes staring into each other, a sense of recognition flashed, he felt it too; the sadness and realization that it was Charles and not Wesley.

"I wanted to marry him," Hattie confessed in a small sob, her eyes filled with tears, her chest heaved, this was the first time she had spoken those words out loud. Waves of sadness and relief washed over her as she buried her head in her father's shoulder.

"I know, I know." his voice weak, yet soft, as tears streamed down his wrinkled, sun-tanned cheeks. "Give your heart time to heal, Charles is patient, he's a good man," her father said after some time had passed. He kissed her head and gave her a squeeze. He tilted her chin upward and looked in her eyes. "I will only ask you this one time. Are you sure you want to do this?"

Hattie drew in a breath, pausing to give serious thought to his question.

"Yes," she said as she nodded her head, "I will marry Charles."

Her head had won. The final decision had been made, searing itself like a branding iron onto her heart.

"Okay, then let's get you to that chapel," her father said with a small smile as he patted her back. The two of them made their way down the stairs and out the front door.

Chapter Twenty-Six

Wesley 1918

Loretta placed the box of sandwiches, a jug of sweet tea and a bottle of whiskey on the counter.

"For your trip," she said, her eyes looking at the box, scanning its contents.

"Thank you, Loretta, I appreciate it," Wes said, his face held a warm smile. He and Loretta had become quite good friends during his time in Chincoteague. After his long trips out on the ocean with Captain Rusty, he would come through the doors of the hotel and she would be sitting at the table in the corner, waiting for him, two cups of hot coffee sitting on the table. They would sit at the table late into the night and share stories, jokes and laughs. Loretta viewed him as a younger brother, he was fun to be around, he was charming and quick witted. He always seemed to have a smile on his face even though his heart ached for Hattie and home. The two friends bonded by loss, a loss that had a way of bringing people together, an understanding that only comes when you have experienced such darkness and loneliness. After the loss of Danny, Loretta had built up a tough exterior that she wore like armor, vowing to keep people out, never allowing people to get in and affect her. But Wes had a way of cutting through the tough exterior. His authenticity allowed her to take the armor off without fear, revealing a kind and compassionate soul that loved her friends and family fiercely. She was the kind of soul that once trust was gained, would take up arms and run head on, into battle with you.

Wes jumped over the counter and wrapped her up in a hug. "I'm going to miss you," Wes told her, his chin resting on the top of her head.

"Oh, you stupid boy!" she said, trying not to let the emotion show in her voice as tears welled in her eyes. "I'm going to miss you too," she continued as she sniffed, bringing her arms up around his back, and patted him friendly. They stepped back from each other, she wiped quickly at her eyes, embarrassed at her emotions. "Now go on, get out of here!" she said, as she waved her hands at him, shooing him towards the door. "You've made a blubbering mess out of me," Loretta said as she followed him to the door.

"I'll bring her back here to visit, she would love the pony penning," Wes said as he turned and faced her.

"Please do! I'll be looking forward to it," Loretta replied with a smile on her face, she held the door for him as he walked out. He turned one last time and gave her a wink as he walked down the dock. She waved and went back inside, as little tears trickled down her rosy cheeks.

The voyage back to Holland Island took two days. The air had started to turn colder as summer made its exit, as autumn swept in. The current was strong against them, pulling them back in the direction they had come from. Captain Rusty ordered the crew to stop a few times along the way to harvest oysters. With every passing hour Wesley's heart pounded harder and harder in his chest, his nerves bubbled up in the pit of his stomach, as he grew more and more impatient. Off in the distance Wes could see land masses that stuck up in the horizon as they made their way up the Chesapeake.

"You're almost home, boy," Captain Rusty said as he patted Wesley on the back. His red cheeks glowing in the sun that sat high above them, a smile spread across his face. Wes drew in a breath and stuck his hands in his pockets and nodded. "I'm sure your family will be happy to have you home," Captain Rusty said, his tone chipper and confident.

Wes took in a deep breath and let it out slowly.

"I'm not sure who or what will be there, or what will be left," Wes replied, his eyes fixed on the horizon, his jaw firm. He refused to let the fear that gripped him completely take over. It wouldn't do any good to him or the crew if he fell apart now. The boat grew closer to the island, and it took everything in him to remain standing. The sight of Holland Island, the place he had now come to call home, was unrecognizable.

Wesley jumped overboard, diving in headfirst. His body hit the water with a splash. The water was chilly, but he didn't care, he had to see what was left, or more importantly, who was left on the island. He swam up to the shore, until his feet could touch the marshy bottom, then he ran. He ran to what was once Hattie's home, the dock was gone, the white picket fence that once surrounded their vegetables and fruits, laid in broken pieces around the yard. The clothesline was tangled in a tree in the distance, its snapped post hanging like a corpse from the branches. The roof looked like an old man's patchy head with spots of the shingles gone. Wes ran to the back door, slammed it open and rushed inside. He stood in the empty kitchen, his chest heaving. His eyes scanned the room, taking in the realization that they were gone. He walked through the living room, empty. He ran up the stairs and through each of the bedrooms, empty. He went back downstairs and left the house through the front door. He took off running again, up Main Street and through what was now a ghost town. Not a single person was on the streets or shops, they sat vacant and quiet.

Wes ran towards Tom's House, stopping when he saw the sight of it. The home was completely gone. He ran a shaking hand through his hair, as he squatted, trying to catch his breath. Moments passed as he took in the sight of where his home was. The one he had planned to spend a life with Hattie. The one he had worked on for weeks making just right was completely gone. He stood, his breathing now normal, and walked towards the shed, it now lay in a heap on the ground. Wes stood and stared at it, the emotions taking over him now. The seagulls called in the distance, as Wes held his face in his hands and wept. He wept for it all, the loss of his father, the loss of Tom, the loss of his home, and the loss of his Oyster Girl, Hattie. Where was she? Was she alright? Would he ever see her again? And what on earth does he do now? He sat, staring out at the bay, his forearms resting on his knees, his hair tousled in the breeze that blew against his face.

The sound of footsteps came up from behind, Captain Rusty plopped himself on the ground next to him with a grunt. The two of them sitting in the same spot Hattie and her mother sat just a few weeks ago.

"I'm sorry son," Captain Rusty said as he patted Wes on the back. Wes nodded and swallowed hard, trying to suppress the lump that was rising in his throat. Silence passed between them, the water slowly lapping at the shore, a heron soared overhead.

Captain Rusty cleared his throat.

"What are you going to do now?" he asked, his eyes squinting at the horizon.

"I don't know," Wes replied, his head lowered, eyes downcast. Captain Rusty drew in a big breath,

"You can work for me until you figure it out?" The question reminded Wes of Old man Tom. He had asked Wes the same question years ago, right here on this property.

Wes felt his walls that he had built so long ago going back up. The walls that Hattie had taken down brick by brick, were now going up at lightning speed, harder and thicker than when he had first built them. He had resolved in that moment to come to grips with what he was now, who he was, he was a drifter. He didn't have a home, nor did he belong anywhere. Never again would he allow himself to be anything more than that. He had opened his heart and felt real love for the first and last time in his life, and he vowed to himself, in that moment, sitting in front of the shack that was now a pile of rubble, the shack where he and Hattie gave themselves to each other, and vowed to never love like that again. Wes drew in a breath, taking in the surroundings, and nodded. He stood and shook off the sand from his pants, and extended a hand to captain Rusty, Wes took his hand and helped pull the old man up. The two of them walked away from Tom's place and towards the vessel that was docked at the vacant town, they walked the entire way without saying a word.

Chapter Twenty-Seven

Eden 1982

Eden, Hudson, her mother, and her grandmother sat at the table on the back porch, making small talk as they ate crab salad sandwiches and drank lemonade.

"So, Hudson, you live across the bay?" Hattie asked.

"Yes Ma'am, in Crisfield," Hudson replied as he took a sip of lemonade.

"That's just above Holland Island," Eden chimed in, Hattie nodded in agreement.

"I heard you used to live on Holland Island back in its heyday," Hudson said, smiling.

"I did. I was born there," Hattie replied slowly, her tone full of nostalgia.

"What was it like?" Hudson asked forwardly, his focus completely on her.

Hattie took a deep breath, paused for a moment, tears filled at the corner of her eyes.

"Well, it had the most beautiful sunsets that made the water glow in reds, pinks, and purples, the birds would sing their songs all year round, the fish that jumped clear out of the water showing off their fat, silver bellies, the dragonflies with a kaleidoscope of colors in their wings." The air in the room stood still as she spoke, the world around her seemed to wake up at her words. Eden stared at her grandmother. She had never heard her talk this way or this much about the island.

Hudson stared at her too, but his gaze held bewilderment. "My grandfather used to say that." Hudson said in almost a whisper as he sat back in his chair, he reached into his pocket and pulled out his pocket watch and set it on the table in front of Eden's grandmother. Her eyes looked down on it, tears streamed down her cheeks as she reached out and delicately touched the antique watch, her fingers remembering as they traced over the familiar flying seagulls.

"Mom, are you ok?" Val asked. Everyone's gaze fixed on Hattie, as she picked up the watch and held it in both of her hands. She brought it to her chest and closed her eyes.

"My Wesley," she said in a whisper. A smile took over her face, the corners of her mouth reaching up, her wrinkles meeting her tears that streamed down her face. Quiet moments passed, allowing Hattie time to reflect.

"You knew him. You knew my grandfather," Hudson stated, low and matter of fact.

Hattie opened her eyes, they glistened, full of love, and full of memories. Memories that up until now had been locked away, tucked down deep inside of her, too painful to relive and talk about, she had banished them to the depths inside of her when she married Charles all those years ago. She moved on with her life, putting the past painfully behind her. But now they were in the forefront of her mind, reborn through a filter of hope because of Hudson. He was living breathing proof that Wesley had lived, that it wasn't over, love did not die on that awful day the hurricane tore apart their island. It had survived. Love had survived.

"Yes, I knew him. I knew him and I loved him. He was my first real love," Hattie replied; her mind now free to wander down memory lane, now knowing that Wes had lived.

Hattie's eyes twinkled and danced as she told them all about her life on the island, how she met Wesley on the water that cold October morning. She told them about their lunch dates, their night out in Cambridge, the live music and dancing, and their first kiss. The memories and details poured out of her like a dam bursting open, unable to hold back any longer. She told them all about the hardships of that winter and the toll that the war had on the country, she told them about the Spanish flu and how her mother had to leave to take care of the soldiers. She told them about the awful hurricane that left the island in shambles, and the gut-wrenching decision to leave and start a new life in Ridge, Maryland, and move into the very house that they were sitting in now. She also told them about the baby.

"You were pregnant?" Val said, searching for clarification.

Hattie took a breath in and let it out slowly, she had never admitted this secret about her past.

"I was, it was the reason I married Charles so quickly after we met. But I miscarried a month after we were married," Hattie said, her eyes that held pain in them now, fell to the floor.

"Oh, Mom. I'm so sorry! That must have been so hard," Val said.

"It was. It was my last piece of Wes, well so I thought," Hattie said with a smile as she motioned her hand towards Hudson.

"How did Grandpa Charles feel about it?" Eden asked.

"He was compassionate through it, but deep down I think he was relieved that he wouldn't have to raise another man's child. We made the choice to stay married despite losing the baby. We grew to love each other, he was a good man and he took care of me, and he gave me you," Hattie said as she patted her daughter's hand. "But there is nothing like your first real love. That is something that remains with you; it marks your heart and soul," Hattie said, as she looked at Eden, and then at Hudson. "I see so much of him in you," Hattie said with a smile as she reached out and squeezed Hudson's hand. Hudson gave her a proud smile in response. "Now it's your turn young man," Hattie said, turning her body in her chair to face him directly. "Tell me, what happened to your grandfather?"

Hudson took a deep breath and began to speak.

"He barely survived the storm; he was picked up by a fishing boat just south of Southern Maryland. Said he would've been swept out to sea had they not found him."

"Oh, my heavens," Hattie said, her voice barely above a whisper.

"The fishing boat took him to Chincoteague Island Virginia, he made a deal with the captain of the boat. If he worked for him then the captain would bring him back to Holland Island."

Hattie brought her hand up to her mouth as Hudson spoke, her heart in her throat, the feelings of that day, the day she sat on shoreline at old man Tom's place and looked out at the bay, willing Wes to come home, rose up inside of her now. "But the Captain took his time getting my grandfather back to Holland Island, way longer than my grandfather had hoped. When he finally made it back, no one was there. He said every single family was gone, the homes, and town were destroyed by the hurricane." Hudson paused and took another sip of his lemonade.

"What did he do after?" Hattie asked her voice full of curiosity.

Chapter Twenty-Eight

Wesley 1918

Annemessex Neck which is now known as Crisfield, Maryland was a beautiful little town, nestled on Tangier sound, an arm of the Chesapeake Bay, reminded Wesley of Ewell in Smith Island where he was born and raised. With its charming fishing docks, shops and quaint homes that were perched along the shoreline. Captain Rusty had taken his crew and Wes to Crisfield after Holland Island. They had quite a lot of Oysters that they had harvested from the bay on their way to Holland Island, and Captain Rusty wanted to get it unloaded, cleaned, shucked, and canned before it went bad. Captain Rusty spent most of his time on his ship going back and forth from Crisfield to Chincoteague Island. Many of the fishermen he knew stayed in one area of the bay, too afraid to venture out into the currents of the sea that could sweep you out if you weren't careful. He liked the challenge and the reward for taking on such a dangerous voyage. The water where the bay met the ocean had always provided a bounty of fresh fish oysters and crabs. Captain Rusty had a shucking shack in each location. He would clean or shuck his harvest and then package it for sale. He made a comfortable living off the bounty that the water provided. He was a fair Captain and paid his men well.

Wesley and the crew spent the entire morning and afternoon unloading, washing, and packaging up their catch, the work was long, dirty and tiresome. Captain Rusty looked over the crew's work when they had finished. Satisfied, he gave them each $20.

"There's a decent boarding house on Norris Harbor Drive, get yourself a hot bath and a warm meal," Captain Rusty said as he handed Wesley his pay.

"Thank you," Wes replied, he put the money in his pocket and headed towards the town. He heard music in the distance. He strained his ear to listen. The popular, familiar tune, "Keep the home fires burning" by James F. Harrison. Wes hummed along as he walked. The song was written about war, but the words hit Wes in a different way now.

"And although your heart is breaking, make it sing this cheery song: Keep the home fires burning, while your hearts are yearning. Though your lads are far away, they dream of home. There's a silver lining through the dark cloud shining. Turn the dark cloud inside out till the boys come home."

Hattie consumed his thoughts, was she alive? And if so, where was she now? Was her heart breaking like his? Or had she moved on, content in whatever life she had now. Wes sang the song to himself as it continued to play from an open restaurant window, changing "lads" to "lass".

That's what I will do, he thought. *I will turn the dark cloud inside out, and go back to Holland Island as much as I can until she returns again.* A small smile took over his face as he opened the door to the boarding house, the aroma of fresh bread, roasting meat and ale filled the air in the room, and for the first time since he stood on the Shore of Holland Island, his heart shattering around him, he felt a sense of peace and purpose.

Wes had slept hard, he had had a hot bath and a good meal and maybe a few too many pints of ale, but the indulgence had felt good. He woke late in the morning, later than he had expected, the sun was high in the sky and the town had been awake for hours, busy with the chores and duties of the day.

Wes hurried to his feet and dressed quickly. He was determined to earn enough money to buy himself another boat since his boat was now in pieces scattered throughout the bay, thanks to the storm. If he was to make it back to Holland Island regularly, then he needed a vessel he could charter on his own. He didn't want to inconvenience Captain Rusty, or any other fisherman for that matter, knowing that they would probably find his endeavor insane or question if he had gone dumb in the head, deciding to keep his plan to himself instead. He made his way down the stairs and to the dining room in the boarding house. Smells of coffee, bacon and pan-fried potatoes lingered in the air.

"Still serving breakfast?" Wes asked, his eyebrows rose in anticipation.

"Sorry love, we've cleaned up from breakfast and we're moving onto lunch," a stout. Middle aged, darker skinned woman said. She had a pleasant face with kind eyes and graying hair that was tied up in a red checkered scarf, small wisps and curls stuck out from under the edges around her forehead and neck.

"I understand. It's my fault for sleeping in," Wes replied with a smile and started to head for the door. The woman looked up and sighed.

"Hold on a minute boy. Dolly, bring any breakfast we have leftover!" she hollered from over her shoulder. "Have a seat young man. Dolly will bring you something to eat," she said with a smile.

"Thank you kindly, Ma'am, I much appreciate it," Wes said as he bowed his head slightly towards the woman and took a seat. A few moments later Dolly appeared from the kitchen holding a plate of bacon, eggs, and some jellied toast. She was a petite girl with fair skin, bright green eyes and wild curly blond hair that fell to her shoulders, she had a blue bandana that she tied into a headband. She looked at the woman with a questioning look. The woman looked at Wes and pointed. Dolly looked at Wes. Wes smiled at her and waved a hand in recognition. She smiled as she walked towards him. Wes couldn't help but smile back at her. She had a childlike innocence that was endearing.

"Here you go Sir," she said as she placed the plate in front of him.

"Sir?!" Wes questioned in protest. "I'm not that old," he said with a chuckle and a friendly smile. "You can call me Wes."

"Pleased to meet you Wes, I'm Dolly, but you already knew that," she said, her cheeks blushing slightly with embarrassment. She looked at the floor and tapped her feet nervously. "Well, I should be getting back to work," she said as she turned slowly and walked past the woman, to the kitchen. The woman looked at her and then at Wes, waiting for a reply from Wes, but he picked up his fork and dove in his breakfast, ravenous from drinking the night before and waking up late. The woman came out from behind the counter, crossed the room and stood in front of Wes. He looked up, startled; he hadn't noticed that she had come to his table.

"She's the only child of Mr. Paul Williams, the owner of this place," she said, stern and serious. Wes stared at her, puzzled by her statement. The woman continued in a stern whisper, slightly bent so she could look him in the eyes. "Her father is fighting in Germany in this God forsaken war. She's the only help I can depend on right now and I don't need her falling for a boy who's going to break her heart. Do you understand me?"

Wes held her gaze, still slightly confused but understanding what she was implying.

"I understand Ma'am. You have nothing to worry about, my heart belongs to another, my intention and desire is to return to her," Wesley said, his eyes were certain and confident.

"Alright then," the woman said, and stood back up straight. "You're welcome to stay here as long as you need to tell you what, if you help me with the heavy shipments and unloading of goods I won't charge you for the room," she said, her eyes softer now, but her voice was still firm. Wes could see that she was a strong woman who was used to hard work and the even harder task of running a business on her own. He could also see the lines that stretched across her forehead and the bags that had taken residence under her eyes.

Wes nodded.

"I would do that, much appreciated. My name is Wesley," he said as he stretched his hand out to shake her hand.

She reached out and shook his hand in return, "Nell."

Over the next few weeks Wesley worked extra hours and took extra shifts after his regular hours working for Captain Rusty, but he reserved every Monday morning to help Nell and Dolly unload the supplies and goods for the boarding house. They had become somewhat of a little family, working together, and even sharing meals together.

Wesley reminded Nell of her family down south. She had made her way up north after her husband passed and children married and left home, moving up north where the jobs and opportunities were better. Nell followed her oldest daughter to Baltimore Maryland, helping her with her household and raising children of her own. Nell met Dolly's mother in the city one afternoon. Nell was selling her homemade jams and pickles at a market, Dolly's mother, Lydia took to her instantly. Nell told her all about how her daughter was fixing to go back down south, to Georgia where they were from and how she hated it down south and didn't want to go, but she had no other options. Dolly's mother offered Nell a job to come work with them at the boarding house that day, and after a few days of consideration, Nell accepted.

Nell enjoyed Wesley's company and his help around the boarding house. It was hard work and she had grown weary in her older age. Her body ached and creaked whenever she moved about, the noises she made whenever she sat down or got up were involuntary now, and she hated every bit of it.

Wesley was a welcome presence not only noticed with Nell, but also with Dolly. Nell saw how the usually meek and mild girl lit up like a firecracker whenever Wes was around. She noticed that Dolly was always up bright and early every Monday morning and waited outside the kitchen in the morning, with a piping cup of coffee for him. Nell had caught Dolly staring at him as he worked at the docks and as he came and went from the house. Dolly even took it upon herself to wash and mend his clothes, folding them neatly and placing them on the end of his bed for when he returned home from a long day's work. Nell's heart couldn't help but ache for Dolly. She knew Wesley's heart belonged to another. He had been vocal about his plans to purchase a boat and make regular trips to Holland Island after the winter months were done. Nell was the closest thing to a mother that Dolly had after her mother passed a few years back due to scarlet fever. Nell's heart ached for Dolly, she could see the coming of the girl's impending broken heart, but she felt unsure that she could do anything about it. She would be the one who would have to help her pick up the pieces and carry on, of that, she was sure.

"Guard your heart my girl," Nell said to Dolly as they peeled potatoes for dinner.

"I don't know what you mean," Dolly answered, her hands had stopped peeling and she looked anxiously at Nell.

"Wesley, you've fallen for him," Nell replied, her eyes fixed on the potato in her hand, a pause lingered after her words. Dolly's fingers nervously played with the scattered potato peels on the counter.

"How do I guard my heart after I've already given it away?" Dolly finally said softly, as sad little tears trickled down her cheeks.

"Oh, my girl," Nell replied, dropping the potato on the counter, pulling Dolly to her and wrapped her up in a big hug. "You've got to tell yourself that you don't need him, that you're better off without him. I know you're fond of the boy, but you've got to be strong like your daddy. Wesley's heart belongs to another girl."

Chapter Twenty-Nine

Dolly 1919

Dolly had been working in the kitchen all morning, she was annoyed and agitated, and the fact that she was agitated made her even more agitated. Wes was going to Holland Island again today. He had purchased his own wharf a few weeks ago from an elderly man in town who was getting out of the fishing business. This was Wesley's third trip to Holland Island, the weather had broken, winter was letting up and spring was on its way in. The bay was alive again. The ducks had laid eggs in their nests. Seagulls took flight in search of food for their young. Turtles swam on the banks, randomly popping their heads in and out above and below the surface of the water.

The first time he had visited the inhabited island, he was gone for three days, and Dolly had been an agitated wreck the entire time he was gone. *What's so great about Holland Island anyway?* she thought, annoyed that a piece of land could get his attention more than she could. For the most part Dolly enjoyed life in Crisfield, she knew just about everyone who lived here, and they knew her. Lydia and Paul's daughter, that's how she was known. She introduced herself to people as Dolly, but they would always reply, "Oh yes, Lydia and Paul's girl." She hadn't minded it, but she was starting to wonder if that was all she would ever be. She hadn't caught the attention of the boys, not like the other girls her age had, who gussied themselves up and sought out the attention of the young men in town. Compared to the other girl's, she was a shadow, she never stood out or made herself known, she was perfectly content to watch the world around her, noticing details and moments but needing to be a part of them, she found comfort in fading into the background.

Wesley was the first young man who had ever caught her attention, the first time she had ever felt something in the way of feelings or wanting to be seen. The first time he smiled at her, her stomach flipped, and the feeling had completely surprised her and took her off guard. He was nothing like the boys she knew in Crisfield, he had depth, passion and a genuine kindness that seemed to be rooted in his bones. She admired the way Wes interacted with people, like everyone was someone. Everyone was seen and known to him. When Wes smiled it seemed like the world around her grew brighter. It was silly, she knew, but that was the best way she could describe it. She hated the fact that she found herself looking for him, trying to be where he was, taking longer than she should with her chores on Monday mornings in the kitchen just so she could be near him, stare at him and make small talk with him. She couldn't help herself, the attraction to him was involuntary and impulsive and she didn't understand it or stop herself from being drawn to him.

The postman burst through the door, a letter in his hand.

"Miss Dolly!" he said, his voice urgent and demanding.

"Yes," Dolly said, her brows furrowed with concern.

The postman took a step towards her, his hands outstretched in her direction.

"A telegram from the frontlines!" he said his eyes wide and concerned as he held it out in front of her.

She had heard of people receiving these telegrams. They were never good news. Death, sickness, and injury were all they ever said. Dolly took a deep breath and swallowed hard as she took the letter from his outstretched hand. She looked at the letter addressed to her. She drew in a deep breath as she tore the envelope open and pulled out the letter.

"Ms. Dorothy Williams.

Sincerely regret inform you 14558 Private Paul D. Williams formerly 6-th battalion, officially reported wounded, and has died.

-Adjutant General."

Dolly folded the letter and put it in her apron pocket. The postman stood, waiting for her to speak.

"Thank you, sir. Good day to you," Dolly said, her voice monotone and void of emotion.

"Ma'am," the postman said as he lifted his hat and placed it back on his head. He slowly turned and walked out the front door. Dolly stood at the counter in the kitchen, the realization of the letter hit her, sudden and hard. Tears streamed down her cheeks, her vision blurred, her hands shook.

"Dolly baby, whatever is the matter?" Nell said as she came into the kitchen, carrying a crate of canned goods from the cellar. Dolly gasped for air as she fell to the floor, she reached into her pocket and pulled out the letter and handed it to Nell. Nell's eyes read the letter; terror took over her face as she read the words. She dropped to the floor beside Dolly and pulled her into her chest, both heaving from their sobs.

The sun was just beginning to set. Dolly filled the kettle with water and set it on the stove. Nell had gone to bed just after dinner, neither of them eating the potatoes and beef that had been slow cooking on the stove all afternoon. She placed a sign in the front window that said, "Closed due to a personal matter." But everyone in town knew by now. Paul Williams had died in the war.

The kettle whistled as steam blew through the spout. She pulled it off the stove and poured it in a mug with a tea bag and a spoonful of sugar and cream. She heard the back door open and shut and then footsteps coming closer, she closed her eyes, feeling a sense of calm knowing who it was. It was Wes. And as much as she hated the effects, he had on her, she also loved the effects he had on her. She felt constantly at war with herself. Going in between feelings of "I want him so bad," to "No, he is in love with someone else and will never love you back." But tonight, she was too tired to argue with herself, she wanted relief, and Wes' presence brought a sense of peace.

She turned and saw his face, relief washed over her at the sight of him. He approached her, concern and empathy filled his face as he grew closer. She wrapped her arms around his torso and buried her head in his chest and breathed in long and deep.

"What happened?" Wes asked, Dolly took a moment before answering, she didn't want to start crying again, for fear that she wouldn't be able to stop. She took a step back from him, her eyes staring at the floor.

"A telegram came today; my father is dead." The words coming out of her mouth didn't seem real, she felt like this was surely a nightmare, and at any moment she would wake up and life would be back to the way it was.

Wes drew in a deep breath and wrapped his arms around her.

"I'm sorry Dolly," he said, his voice low and comforting, Wes knew all too well the crippling feeling of loss. It was a monster that ripped open your heart without warning, leaving you broken and exposed, unable to breathe. And then, just when you regained composure, ripped you open again.

The months that followed the death of Dolly's father were long and hard. The town held a small ceremony and burial at the church and cemetery in town. Nell and Wesley had taken on a lot of the responsibilities of the boarding house, trying to ease the burden of grief that lingered over Dolly. Nell tried to give Dolly time to be alone, to take walks at the shoreline and ride her bike through town.

"Time is the best medicine." Nell had told Dolly the morning after the postman delivered the letter. Wes hadn't gone back to Holland Island since the news of Dolly's father. He had come to know Nell and Dolly very well and had considered them like family, he now felt responsible for the livelihood of these two women. It had been months since the news of Dolly's father's passing, and Wes was preparing to go to Holland Island in the morning. He missed it, he felt lost, now more than ever. He longed for home and for Hattie. He wanted to hold her and tell her all about what had happened, about the stress that he now felt with Dolly, Nell and the upkeep of the boarding house.

Wes wrapped up a few slices of fresh baked bread, a small jar of pickles and a can of crabmeat and placed it in his lunch tin. Dolly had gone to bed after dinner. Her eyes always held dark circles underneath, Nell had insisted that she go to bed after dinner every night with a cup of chamomile tea.

"What are you packing up for?" Nell's voice said from behind him, inquisitive but kind.

Wes turned his head to look at her.

"I'm heading to Holland Island tomorrow, not sure how long I'll be gone," he said, his tone low and sure.

Nell's eyes fell to the floor. She drew in a deep breath and came up beside him. She cupped his face in her hands and looked him straight in the eyes.

"Now listen to me son, I know your heart yearns for another, but she's gone. You've got to come to grips with it. All this wasting time going to visit that abandoned place is only going to break your heart and kill your soul. You're looking for a ghost when there's a perfectly good girl right here in Crisfield that loves you."

Wes kept his eyes on hers, his brows furrowed in confusion.

"You're a bit old for me don't you think?" Wes said, a small smile taking over his face.

"Oh hush your mouth. I'm talking about Dolly you dummy," she said as she playfully slapped his shoulder. "I know I told you to stay away from her, but the truth of the matter is, she needs you, we need you. Her daddy is dead and she's an unmarried 20-year-old young lady. The government will not allow her to own and operate this property; they will come and take it from us. You know that. She'll be a beggar in the streets, and I'll have to go south, back to them God forsaken swamps and my shack of a home in Georgia."

Wesley's eyes fell to the floor. Nell drew in a breath and let out a long sigh and continued.

"I know you're a good man, I'm asking you to find it in your heart to marry the girl and keep this boarding house in business. It's all we have."

Chapter Thirty

Hattie 1982

"He married Dolly, didn't he?" Hattie said, her eyes glistening in the afternoon sun.

"Yes Ma'am," Hudson replied, his voice empathetic but not apologetic. Hattie smiled as she looked out at the backyard; her eyes scanned the vegetable garden and the beds of flowers that were in full summer bloom. Two white butterflies twirled and danced in the air; a dove softly cooed in the distance.

"I would expect nothing less, he was a good man. Seems like we both did what needed to be done at the time," Hattie said with a soft smile as she patted Hudson's hand.

"He and Dolly stayed and lived in Crisfield. They turned the boarding house into a bed and breakfast with a nice dining area; my grandpa did most of the work himself. Then when they had my mom, they made it a restaurant only and lived in the upstairs rooms," Hudson said, his words very matter of fact.

Hattie nodded her head and smiled. "That sounds like a wonderful life."

"My grandpa started going back to Holland Island when I was 2 years old, he said that he would pick me up from my parents' house and take me out all afternoon. We explored every inch of the island together. It was our favorite place, we'd fish, harvest oysters, watch the herons and pelicans raise their young. He taught me everything I know about the Bay and the wildlife that lives in and around it. After my Grandma Dolly passed away, our trips to the island became more infrequent. He was getting older, and his mind was getting away from him, well, that's what my mom said. Now he doesn't really remember anything, just sits in his chair in his room or on the porch and stares out at the water." Hudson said with a sigh, his eyes falling to the floor.

"He's still alive?!" Eden said, her voice pitched in shock. All three women stared at Hudson: eyes wide with curiosity.

"Yes, but he's not the same, he has dementia and doesn't remember me or even his own kids most of the time." Hudson said, his shoulders raised and his hands up, suddenly feeling the need to defend himself.

"All this time! I can't believe you never told me he was still alive!" Eden said, a bit dramatically, rising to her feet, her arms flailed in the air.

"Eden dear, calm down, it's alright," Hattie said and motioned for her to sit back down. Eden took a deep breath and sat back down at the table; Hattie patted her on the leg.

"Is he still in Crisfield?" Hattie asked, looking at Hudson.

"Yes," Hudson said, dumbfounded. Everyone seemed to take a breath then, allowing a calm to come over the room.

"I have an idea," Eden said, her eyes wide, sparkling with mischief and hope. She turned to her grandmother and took her wrinkled hands in hers, "I bring you to Holland Island and Hudson brings his grandfather. The two of you at Holland Island, together again, back where it all started." Eden's eyes bounced between Hattie's and Hudson's searching their faces for a reaction to her idea.

"I don't know if my grandfather would be able to do that, I told you, he barely remembers who anyone is or even who he is," Hudson said, his tone full of doubt.

"But maybe if he was there, in the place that he loved more than anywhere in the world, and he was with Hattie, maybe it would bring his mind back, if even for a moment, wouldn't it be worth a shot?" Eden said, her eyes pleading with the two of them.

Hattie's gaze was out the window now, her eyes fixed in the direction of Holland Island. "I haven't been back since the day I was 18, his child in my womb and his ring on my finger." Hattie said, her voice barely louder than a whisper. A silence hung in the air, her words hitting them each deeply. Val set her hand on Eden's shoulder, a silent way of telling her daughter to not push it any further. Eden reached in her pocket and pulled out the pearl ring, the one she had found in the wooden trunk in the attic and set it down on the table in front of her grandmother.

"He's alive," Eden said, her eyes fixed on her grandmother. Hattie looked at the ring, her mouth slightly parted, she drew in a breath, her eyes brimmed with tears as she reached out, picked up the ring and slid it on her finger.

Eden was up early that following Saturday. She loaded the boat with a picnic blanket, a cooler of drinks, and sandwiches. She didn't know if Hudson would be able to convince his grandfather to meet them at Holland Island today at noon, but she was determined to try. The water lapped against the side of the boat in a nervous rhythm, as if it were anticipating the venture that they were about to embark on.

Eden had to beg for permission from Melanie's father to use the boat again after her overnight rendezvous the last time she borrowed it. Melanie had also pleaded with her on Eden's behalf, she wanted to go along and promised her father that they would be extremely careful, and Eden's mom was going with them this time. Melanie's father had eventually given in.

Melanie had suspected that her father had a crush on Val. She caught him staring and smiling a few times when they had seen each other at the grocery store or running errands.

"Why don't you ask her out?" Melanie said one afternoon after her father and Val had run into each other in town.

Her bluntness took him off guard.

"I... I don't know what or who you're talking about," he had responded, fumbling over his words like an embarrassed schoolboy.

"Dad, come on. You know who I'm talking about. Val, Eden's mom," Melanie replied, her words dripping in sass and her eyes slightly rolling.

"I don't think she would say yes, besides, it's your best friend's mom. It would be too weird." He said, his white knuckles gripped the steering wheel, he shook his head as if to dismiss the conversation. Melanie looked at him hard, eyes squinting, but he kept his eyes on the road and turned up the radio, implying that the conversation was over. Melanie crossed her arms and looked forward, *Men*, she thought as she rolled her eyes.

Melanie and her father walked down the dock towards Eden; Melanie's eyes were bright and full of excitement. She ran ahead of her father and jumped in the boat.

"Can you believe this is happening?!" Melanie said to Eden as she gripped her shoulders and gave her a playful shake.

"I know! Isn't it crazy!?" Eden replied. Her wide smile took over her entire face.

"Where are your mom and grandma?" Melanie asked, looking around the dock and grassy area for them.

"They're coming, I couldn't wait any longer, I had to get out here." Eden replied as she put the picnic blanket and a stack of towels under the bench seat in the back of the boat. Melanie's father, Chris, was at the boat now, loading a small cooler, a bag of snacks and towels.

"Good morning, Eden." Chris said with a smile, he opened his arms for a hug.

"Hello Mr. Chris, thank you for letting us take the boat out again," Eden said as she went in for a hug.

"Of course, when I heard the story about your grandmother and the man she knew from Holland Island, I couldn't resist." Chris said as he released her from his hug. Footsteps sounded on the dock in the distance, the boards creaked and groaned as Val and Hattie made their way down the dock and towards the boat.

"Good morning, ladies!" Chris called out.

"Good morning!" Val replied, her eyes bright blue, reflecting the water that glistened and shimmered around her.

My goodness, she was beautiful, Chris thought. Chris helped the two women in the boat, untied the lines and started the engine. Eden took a seat beside her grandmother.

"Are you doing alright?" Eden asked as she patted her grandmother's leg. Hattie was dressed in a yellow sundress; her hair was in a long silver-white braid that fell down her back and was tied off with the faded satin ribbon. Small curls fell around her forehead and sides of her face. The wind played with her hair, sending them dancing around her face. She looked beautiful, full of life and hope, but also nostalgic, the lines in her forehead and around her mouth were worn from a lifetime of moments and emotions.

"I am. I never imagined I would return to Holland Island after all these years, but I feel alive again, thank you for that," Hattie said as she kissed the side of Eden's head. Eden smiled and drew in a deep breath through her nose, taking in the salty, fishy scented melody of the bay.

An entire lifetime had been unveiled over the past week. So much had come to light since either of them was out on these waters. Hattie and Eden stared straight ahead as they made their way out into the water, holding hands as they returned to the bay.

Chapter Thirty-One

Wesley 1982

His feet were unsteady beneath him. He shuffled as he walked to his chair on the front porch. His daughter in law held his elbow as he lowered himself into the chair. Deep wrinkles spread across his tanned fore- head, years of life on the water showed on his face, arms and hands. His eyes, the color of storm clouds, deep and full, barely blinked in the sunlight.

"Hudson, I don't think it's a good idea, he can barely get around without constant help, what if he loses his balance and falls overboard?" Hudson's mother said in a whisper over her shoulder.

"I'll make sure he's wearing a life vest," Hudson said with a smirk.

"Hudson!" his mother scolded and smacked him playfully. "I'm serious! I can't go with you, you know I get seasick," his mother replied, concern filled every word.

"He's not a stranger to the water, he spent his whole life on the water, his sea legs will come back, I really think it would do him some good to go out there. Trust me. I won't let anything happen to him."

His mother sighed heavily.

"Alright, but if anything happens to him, it's on you." She rubbed her temples, leaned down and looked Wes in the eyes and put her hand on his shoulder. "Hudson is taking you out on the water, to visit Holland Island," she said, searching his face for any signs of recognition. Wes' eyes squinted slightly but remained focused on the bay. He drew in a long breath but said nothing. Hudson's mother stood straight and shot Hudson a look of concern.

"It'll be fine," Hudson said, his voice was just slightly louder than a whisper.

Hudson spent the next 30 minutes loading his boat, pulled out a life jacket for his grandfather and started it up. The sun was high and hot.

"Make sure you bring plenty of water and sunscreen," his mother said sternly as he packed the bag for the day. Hudson pulled Wesley to his feet and gave him a minute to steady himself.

"Ready for an adventure?" Hudson asked him with a smile. Wesley turned and looked at him, a flicker of excitement in his eyes, but he said nothing. The two of them slowly made their way down the front steps, across the dock and into the boat. The boat swayed back and forth from the weight of the two of them as they got in, Hudson placed the life jacket over his grandfather's head and secured it around his waist, just the way his grandfather once did for him when he was a little boy. The boat moved forward as Hudson put the throttle down, he looked sideways at his grandfather as he picked up speed, Wes' eyes sparkled, the corners of his eyes crinkled as he gave a small smile. Little waves stretched out beside them as they parted the water, venturing further out into the open bay. The gulls flew overhead, squawking and squalling, as if they were welcoming their old friend back to the water, back to his home. Wesley's eyes were bright and light, taking in the sounds, smells, and scenes of the Chesapeake. Hudson gave out a laugh as he looked at his grandfather, a wide smile on his face, his gray hair that whipped in the wind, he was back, even if it was only a moment, he saw his grandfather again, the man who had first shown him the beauty and wonder of this place, the man who taught him how to drive a boat, and taught him all about tides and currents, how to spot sandbars in the middle of the open water and how weather can change in an instant. Hudson could see the spark and twinkle of his grandfather, Wesley, the oysterman from Smith Island, the boy who grew up in and on the water alongside his father, then becoming a man who made a living from the wildlife that inhabited the waters and lived along the bay floor, the man who felt more comfortable on the water than on the land. This water took so much life and love from him, but also gave him love and life and purpose. And in that moment, Hudson saw it all displayed across his grandfather's face, radiant joy and unbelievable sorrow, the Chesapeake Bay.

The island came into view, the weathered white house that stuck out of the water like a foreign object, the last remaining building and witness of the town and life that was once Holland Island. Fat, gray pelicans sat peacefully on its roofline, basking in the sun, as if nothing about the house was odd or frail at all. The faded and chipped paint was even more visible now with its large patches of weathered wood. The crumbling foundation still held up the home, refusing to give in despite the missing stones and deteriorating mortar. And yet, somehow, the home still held hope, standing on the fading land out among the water as if to say, "I'm still here, and my stories still live on."

Wesley tried to stand to his feet, his eyes recognizing the structure and land. Hudson stopped the boat and raced to his grandfather's side, holding onto his arm to steady him.

"That's Hattie's house," Wesley said, his voice low and gravely. Hudson's eyes grew wide. His grandfather had not spoken a word in months.

"What did you say?" Hudson asked, tilting his head low and trying to make eye contact with him. Wesley stood straight up, his feet solid beneath him, and stretched his arm out, pointing in the direction of the white house.

"That's Hattie's house!" Wesley said again, clear and loud in Hudson's face. Hudson looked at the house, then back at his grandfather then back at the house again, his mind desperately trying to comprehend this moment. His grandfather, who hadn't spoken a word and at times not remembering who his family was, was now recognizing a home that he had known 65 years ago, and a girl, whom he had known and loved, lived in it. Hudson pulled the boat up on the shoreline and helped his grandfather out, taking off his life jacket and throwing it back in the boat.

The past flooded Wesley now, standing in the presence of the weathered home, surrounded by the life he had once lived. He blinked his watery eyes and spun slowly around, the memories and images playing in reels around him. The buildings were resurrected in his memory and stood in front of him. The people from years ago were alive, walking through town and sitting on their front porches like they once were, alive and real. *Wait, were they? Or was his mind playing tricks on him again? Was that Hattie?* Wesley thought as he squinted his eyes and rubbed them. She was standing on the steps of her home in a sundress. Her silver hair was tied in a long braid with a faded yellow satin ribbon, the one he had given her in the oyster can before he went to Roanoke. Silver, wild curls flew around her face. Her eyes sparkled in the sunlight. Long, deep wrinkles framed her eyes as she smiled at the sight of him. She was real, and she was here.

His legs wobbled as made his way up the beach and onto the grass leading to the home. Hattie ran down the weathered wooden steps towards him, the years that had passed disappearing like snow in the warmth of the sun. The memories and feelings of all those years ago flooded her heart, her eyes filled with tears as she closed the distance between them. She stopped in front of him, out of breath but full of wonder and awe. She reached a wrinkled hand up to his face. He took her hand in his as she brushed his tanned cheek. Tears streamed down their cheeks as he pulled her into him, the side of her face pressed against his chest, the familiar comfort of him, his smell washing over her. They were home. After all these years, they were together.

Their love had returned to the bay.

Epilogue

The sun was just beginning to set, casting a warm glow on the yard. Shades of pinks and purples spread across the sky, showing off the beauty of summer's exit and autumn's impending arrival. There was a slight chill in the air, Wesley wrapped a wool blanket around Hattie's shoulders and slowly lowered himself, sitting next to her on the porch swing. She held his hand as her feet lightly pushed off the porch floorboards, rocking them back and forth. She placed her head on Wesley's shoulder, allowing herself to sink into him. Hudson and Eden threw the Frisbee in the yard, laughing and flirting.

"Ah, young love," Hattie said softly.

"Beautiful and terrifying," Wesley said, the two of them laughed at that. "Where's your daughter tonight?" Wes asked.

"She's on a date with Chris, Melanie's father," Hattie said with a mischievously playful smile.

Eden ran up onto the porch, smiling and out of breath.

"Hudson wants to take us back to Holland Island tomorrow, it might be the last warm day we have before fall," Eden said in between breaths.

"Well then I suppose we should go, don't you?" Hattie said, turning her head up to look at Wes, her brows raised in question.

"I suppose we should," Wes replied, his eyes glistening as he smiled at her, and kissed the top of her head.

Eden flew off the porch, descending to the ground in one long jump.

"They said yes! We can go back to Holland Island," she hollered to Hudson. Her voice echoed and carried off among the katydids and bullfrogs, and in the distance a seagull called out.

THE END

Author Notes

The picture on the front of the book was the last house standing on Holland Island. It stood against the wind and waves until 2010, when it finally crumbled into the bay. To this day, there is almost an entire island underwater. The grave-stone for Effie Lee Wilson was an actual gravestone that was located in a family cemetery on the island. It is the only thing remaining above water.

Ulman Owens was an actual lighthouse keeper at the Holland Bar lighthouse. He was a known womanizer and was found dead in his kitchen in the lighthouse in 1931. There was a gruesome scene and a bloody butcher knife by his body, but they ruled his death was due to natural causes. Seriously, you should look it up, it's crazy.

The character Loretta is dedicated to and inspired by Loretta Walsh. Loretta was the first woman to serve in the U.S. armed forces in a non-nursing role when she enlisted in the Navy Reserve on March 17, 1917.

The stories and names of the characters in this book are not real. However, it is likely that many of the people and families who lived on the island during the early 1900s experienced many of the circumstances in this book. If you're interested in learning more about Holland Island and its efforts to save it, there is a YouTube video made by lm2857 titled Holland Island Research; I highly recommend you check it out!

Thank you for taking the time to read this story, it is very near and dear to my heart and I hope that you felt that as you read about Hattie and Wes. I also hope that you were inspired and learned something that you may have never known before.

For more information on other books written by Hannah Westley go to Hannahwestley.com

Hannah Westley

Hannah Westley was born and raised in rural
Maryland. She grew up with her six brothers and
sisters. She spent summers on her dad's boat on the
Chesapeake Bay and came to love the areas and
islands in and around it.

She still resides in Maryland with her husband, Jeffrey, and a blended family of seven. She is a singer/songwriter as well, you can most likely find her playing in a bar in the Frederick County area on Thursday evenings and weekends.

To find more information about her and her music, you can visit hannahmichelle.com